The Spybot Invasion

Read all the books in the
**TOM SWIFT INVENTORS'
ACADEMY** series!

The Drone Pursuit
The Sonic Breach
Restricted Access
The Virtual Vandal
The Spybot Invasion

TOM SWIFT
INVENTORS' ACADEMY

-BOOK 5-
The Spybot Invasion

VICTOR APPLETON

Aladdin
NEW YORK LONDON TORONTO SYDNEY NEW DELHI

ALADDIN

An imprint of Simon & Schuster Children's Publishing Division
1230 Avenue of the Americas, New York, New York 10020
First Aladdin hardcover edition July 2020
Text copyright © 2020 by Simon & Schuster, Inc.
Jacket illustration copyright © 2020 by Kevin Keele
TOM SWIFT, TOM SWIFT INVENTORS' ACADEMY, and related logos are trademarks of Simon & Schuster, Inc.
Also available in an Aladdin paperback edition.
All rights reserved, including the right of reproduction in whole or in part in any form.
ALADDIN and related logo are registered trademarks of Simon & Schuster, Inc.
For information about special discounts for bulk purchases, please contact Simon & Schuster Special Sales at 1-866-506-1949 or business@simonandschuster.com.
The Simon & Schuster Speakers Bureau can bring authors to your live event.
For more information or to book an event contact the Simon & Schuster Speakers Bureau at 1-866-248-3049 or visit our website at www.simonspeakers.com.
Jacket designed by Heather Palisi
Interior designed by Mike Rosamilia
The text of this book was set in Adobe Caslon Pro.
Manufactured in the United States of America 0620 BVG
10 9 8 7 6 5 4 3 2 1
Library of Congress Cataloging-in-Publication Data 2019949299
ISBN 978-1-5344-5120-9 (hc)
ISBN 978-1-5344-5119-3 (pbk)
ISBN 978-1-5344-5121-6 (eBook)

Contents

The Gravitation Acceleration

"I KNOW I'M NOT THE ONE WHO USUALLY SAYS this, Tom," Noah said. "But are you sure this is a good idea?"

"No problem," I replied confidently. I strapped the last section onto my forearm. "It worked just fine on the test dummy."

"But that was only off my back deck," Noah explained. "This is a whole flight of stairs."

As I stood on the third-floor landing and looked into the stairwell, I realized my best friend *might* have a point. You see, I was about to test our latest invention—

a full-body airbag—by flinging myself down a flight of stairs. You know how there are airbags in cars? Well, this would be a portable one that cyclists and motorcyclists could wear. It was a whole suit made up of several components that covered my entire body. Straps and wires snaked up my arms and legs, connecting several sections of clear plastic. It kind of looked like a weird, futuristic pants-and-jacket set.

"The Wright brothers didn't use a dummy," I told Noah.

"No, but they weren't risking breaking their necks," Noah replied. "Wait a minute. I guess they were."

"Dude, don't worry," I said. "I have complete confidence in your software."

Noah Newton was a programming genius. Using an old smartphone (which already had built-in motion sensors), Noah had written a program that would detect when I was falling. Then it would activate several tiny CO_2 canisters spread throughout the special outfit I had designed.

"Wait a minute," Noah said, digging through his pocket. He pulled out his phone. "We need a video record of this."

"I don't think that's going to be a problem," I said, nodding past him.

Several academy students were already gathering behind him with their phones at the ready.

That was the cool thing about our school—you never knew what could happen from one day to the next. Well, I guess that's just *one* of the cool things about our school. We've had an all-out robot war tournament for our robotics class. Our programming teacher actually encourages us to create apps for phones and tablets for extra credit. And yes, one of the students could perform a crazy experiment in the halls (or stairwells) at any moment. That's the Swift Academy of Science and Technology for you.

Oh, and yeah, I share a name with the school. My father, Tom Swift Sr., founded the academy with the profits from his next-door company, Swift Enterprises. Most people think it's cool, but honestly, I usually wished people forgot about my connection to the school. I don't want any special treatment, positive or negative. I just want to be an ordinary student like everyone else. Okay, I was about to fling myself down a set of stairs for science, but you know what? That is kind of ordinary for our school.

3

I leaned over the railing and gazed at the second-floor landing. "Sam? Amy? All clear down there?"

Sam poked her head out and adjusted her glasses. "I still think you're nuts, Swift," she called back up. "But yeah, it's all clear."

Samantha Watson and Amy Hsu were blocking off the stairs on the second floor. Granted, there wasn't much traffic in the stairwells during lunch hour, but you could never be too careful. I was wearing an airbag suit for *my* protection. Any unsuspecting student coming up the stairs wouldn't be.

Sam and Amy were good friends with Noah and me and were the last two members of the "formidable foursome," as my dad liked to call us. Like all the other academy students, they were both crazy smart. Personally, I thought they were two of the smartest students in the school.

I'm not a genius, or child prodigy by any means. I just enjoy coming up with cool inventions. Of course, as I looked down at the stairs below, and then back at the flimsy plastic covering my body, I was questioning my intelligence a bit.

Our idea wasn't completely new. Someone had already

invented an inflatable airbag helmet for cyclists. Then, of course, there were avalanche airbags, which were special backpacks that skiers wore in avalanche-prone environments. If someone was caught in an avalanche, the backpack would expand to keep them from being crushed beneath several feet of heavy snow. Our idea was a combination of the two. It had the size of the avalanche bag yet the formfitting shape of the airbag helmet. Except our airbags covered the entire body, not just the head.

"Well?" Sam asked from below. "Did you change your mind?" She crossed her arms and looked up with a skeptical expression. "It's all right if you did, you know."

I shook my head and eased up to the first step. "Nope," I replied. "We're still a go."

Now, don't get me wrong. I'm not *completely* reckless. You see, I was sure the motion sensors and Noah's program would work. But . . . just in case they didn't, I had a backup plan. I reached into a jacket pocket and pulled out a small tethered thumb switch. I could always activate the airbags manually if needed.

"Okay," I said. "Here goes . . ." I slowly leaned forward.

5

"Uh, Tom," Noah said. "Maybe we should run some more tests first...."

But it was too late. There was no stopping now. I bent my knees and elbows as I saw the stairs flying up toward my face. My heart beat faster, my body tensed, and I almost panicked and pressed the button. My thumb hovered over the switch.

BAFF!

The airbags inflated all over my body before I could press the button. A grin stretched across my face as I felt my limbs stiffen, the airbags keeping me completely immobile from head to toe. And when my body hit the first step, I barely felt the impact.

"Yes!" Noah shouted from above.

"It worked?" came Sam's voice from below.

"Oh yeah," replied Noah.

I was too busy laughing to add to Noah's reply as I bounced harmlessly down the stairs. I was too immobile to steer, so I just went with it and tried to enjoy the bouncy roller-coaster ride. But when I hit the back wall and was supposed to stop, I ended up rebounding and began bouncing down the second set of stairs.

"Coming to you, Sam!" Noah shouted.

Have you ever worn one of those inflatable sumo-wrestler suits? The kind you and a friend wear and then bounce into each other? Well, I hadn't, but I imagine that's what this felt like. You take up way more space than you're used to, and all the while looking kind of silly.

My world was spinning as I tumbled down the next flight of stairs. I only caught blurry glimpses of Sam's wide eyes and the crowd of students behind her holding up their phones. I must've looked something like a clear beach ball with a boy suspended inside.

Sam turned to the crowd behind her and spread her arms wide. "Okay, everyone, get back!"

She ushered the students away from the second-floor landing as I approached. I held my breath. It felt like I was gathering enough momentum to bounce off the landing and into the hallway itself. The last thing I wanted was to knock down a bunch of students as if they were bowling pins.

Noah and I didn't really have a plan to stop my descent. That was kind of my thing: Act first and figure the rest out later. I had assumed I would stop when I hit the first wall at the bottom of the first flight.

7

As I bounced off the last step, I felt a hard jerk to one side. I must've hit the corner of the step at just the wrong angle, because I didn't slide down the second-floor hallway as I thought I would. As embarrassing as that would've been, at least I would've stopped. No, I flew toward the stairwell wall, bounced off it, and began tumbling down the *next* flight of steps.

"What are you doing?" Sam asked.

"Can't . . . steer," I said as I bounded down the stairs.

Okay, this wasn't so fun anymore. My stomach was spinning almost as much as I was. I would be lucky to hold down breakfast when this was all over.

"Look . . . out . . . !" I said as I bounced down toward the next floor.

None of us had anticipated going this far, so we didn't have anyone holding back foot traffic coming up from the first floor. Terry Stephenson and Jamal Watts both hugged the wall as I tumbled past them. I would've felt embarrassed if my nausea wasn't overshadowing everything else.

I kept my hands in fists most of the time to keep from breaking one of my fingers. But whenever I thought it was safe, I reached out with my hand, trying to grab anything to slow me down—the handrail, the wall, anything.

Luckily, I didn't bounce off the landing between the first and second floor. I hit the angle just right and was almost standing straight up when I finally came to a stop against the wall. However, not being able to move, I couldn't catch my balance and I fell onto my back. It didn't hurt, though. In fact, nothing on my body hurt. I had just fallen almost three flights of stairs and I would've bet that I didn't have a single bruise.

My stomach was a different matter. It continued to turn as I lay there looking at an upside-down world. I hoped someone had the decency to turn me over if I started to hurl.

I spotted two people running up to me. I don't know if it was my nausea or the fact that everything was upside down, but I didn't recognize them at first. A girl with long black hair ran up the stairs, followed by a woman with her long brown hair pulled back into a ponytail.

"Tom! Are you all right?" the girl asked. My vision cleared and I realized that it was my friend Amy. Sam and Noah ran down the stairs followed by what seemed like the rest of the academy students.

"Just a little . . . nauseated," I replied.

The woman reached down and squeezed the air-bag surrounding my left arm. "How do you deflate this thing?" the woman asked. I realized that it was the school nurse, Ms. Ramos.

"It was supposed to deflate after the first step," I said.

Ms. Ramos rolled her eyes and nodded to Noah and Sam. "All right, you two. Help us get him to my office."

I was too nauseated to argue.

The Recovery
Discovery

"ARE YOU SURE YOU'RE NOT GOING TO BE SICK?"
Ms. Ramos asked. She held out a kidney-shaped plastic
basin.

I waved it away with the fingers on my right hand.
"No, I'm okay." Even though I still felt a little queasy,
the container looked way too small to do any good if I
got sick.

I sat hunched over on the edge of the exam table in
the nurse's office. My entire airbag suit was still inflated,
so I was more propped on the edge than sitting.

Ms. Ramos eyed me suspiciously as she pulled out

a pair of medical shears. "You still look a little green." She took the shears and carefully cut the clear plastic airbag helmet surrounding most of my head. Air hissed out as she moved on to my right arm. Once she pulled the deflated plastic away from my body, she produced an instant cold pack. She squeezed the pack and gave it a shake before placing it into my free hand. "Hold this to your forehead," she said. "It'll help."

As I placed the cool pack against my skin, Ms. Ramos put the shears to work again. She carefully deflated more airbag sections, and I let out a deep breath. The ice pack did work; I felt less nauseated.

"What were you thinking, Tom?" Ms. Ramos asked. "You could've seriously hurt yourself."

"We already tested it on a dummy," I explained. "It was time to test it on a real person."

Ms. Ramos shook her head. "Do you remember when I went to every class and showed you how to perform CPR?"

"Yeah?" I said. I didn't know where she was going with this.

She continued to deflate more airbags. "Well, I didn't demonstrate CPR on real people, did I?"

"No," I replied. "You used that dummy."

"Exactly," she said. "You don't test things like this on real people. I've actually performed CPR on a real person once, and even though it saved his life, it hurt him, too."

"You've done CPR for real?" I asked. "When was that?"

Ms. Ramos continued to free me from my inflated airbags. "When I was the nurse at my last school, a man came to speak to the students. Unfortunately, his heart stopped and I had to perform CPR on him until the ambulance arrived."

"Wow," I said. "So, you saved his life?"

Ms. Ramos shook her head. "Yes, but that's not the point." She aimed the shears at me. "After everything he went through, the bruising from my chest compressions took the longest to heal."

"Yeah, but still," I said. "You saved his life. That must've felt pretty good."

Ms. Ramos smiled. "At the time it was terrifying. But now, yeah, it does feel good."

I couldn't even imagine doing something as big as saving someone's life. Sure, Ms. Ramos had always done a great job taking care of us. Just last month she had performed the Heimlich maneuver on Charlie Wells when he was choking in the school cafeteria. But I can imagine that in a school like the academy, you'd never know what kind of injury a school nurse could run across. With everyone working on so many different inventions, experiments, and unusual school projects, Ms. Ramos might be treating small burns one day and minor frostbite the next. It felt . . . nice, having someone like her around.

"I want to save someone's life," I said, almost without thinking.

Ms. Ramos raised an eyebrow and paused her airbag-suit removal.

"I—I mean," I stammered. "I think it would be cool to come up with an invention that could save someone's life."

She deflated the last part of my airbag suit. "Well, you're off to a good start," she said, then pointed to my arm. "These sections on your arms and legs are already similar to inflatable splints."

"That's a thing already?" I asked.

"Sure," she replied. "For when someone breaks an

arm or a leg. You blow the splint up and it keeps the limb immobile so you can move the patient."

"Oh," I said. "I guess I'll have to come up with something else."

She aimed her finger at me. "Promise me that you won't go testing your inventions on yourself again."

I nodded. "I promise."

I held up my arm and looked at the tattered remains of my airbag suit. It seemed kind of pathetic now, but I wondered if this could be my lifesaving invention. How cool would that be? Maybe it would save someone in a motorcycle crash. Or maybe an experimental test pilot could use it.

But this thing had a long way to go. I tugged at one of the clear strips hanging from my wrist. *It's back to the drawing board*, as my dad would say. Not only did this thing not deflate when it was supposed to, but there are tons of different scenarios that I'd have to account for to trigger such a device. I'd have to think of some other way to come up with a lifesaving invention. My mind raced with concepts and ideas.

Ms. Ramos put away the shears and reached out for my chin. She gently held it, turning my head slightly.

"Your color is almost back to normal. How do you feel?"

"Just a little queasy," I said. I began to stand. "I'll be fine."

The nurse placed a firm hand on my shoulder. "I think you should wait here just a bit longer. Want me to call your father?"

My eyes widened. "No!" What was she doing? I thought she wanted my nausea to pass, not make it worse. "I mean, he'll find out about everything soon enough. No sense in ruining his day."

And my day, too, I thought.

She smiled and tousled my hair. "Okay, why don't you relax and lie back for a few minutes to let your stomach settle?"

I did as she instructed and closed my eyes. The cold pack felt soothing and the nausea continued to fade into nothingness. I heard Ms. Ramos milling around in her office before she left the room, and I lay alone in silence.

I tried to think of other inventions that could possibly save lives. I dove headfirst into the middle of one of my favorite parts of inventing—brainstorming. Here there were no wrong answers, no stupid ideas, and no limits. Could I invent a lifesaving drug? That would require years of medical school, but it was a possibility. Or I could always go the engineering route. Maybe I could create some sort of new surgical tool.

I opened my eyes and gazed about her office. Two framed photographs sat on her nearby desk. One showed a young boy and a girl—maybe eight or nine years old. The other photo showed a grinning little girl who was almost a toddler, and I felt myself smiling back at her as she proudly stood for what might be one of the first times. These must've been Ms. Ramos's kids. I wondered if they realized just how cool their mom really was.

My smile faded when I spotted an odd plastic figurine next to the photos. It had a squat, cartoonish body and an oversize head, with two batlike ears pointing straight up. Its two devilish eyes seemed to stare back at me. But what was most unsettling was its devious expression, with its mouth in the shape of a circle as if it were saying, *Oooooh*.

A small shiver went through my body. I reached over and spun the creepy figurine around so it faced the wall.

3

The Reiteration Equation

MS. RAMOS CUT ME LOOSE IN TIME TO MAKE THE second half of my physics class. I was no longer nauseated but I decided to skip the stairs for the time being. I headed to the elevator instead. I stepped inside and pressed the button for the third floor.

"Hold the door, please," came a voice from the corridor.

It was Tristan Caudle. I held back the doors as he glided into the elevator in his wheelchair. Jake Mahaley jogged in behind him. I expected to get some ribbing for my tumble down the stairs, but we rode the elevator up in silence.

"I didn't say anything," Jacob said suddenly. "I swear."

"Well then how else did he find out?" Tristan snapped back.

I nervously took half a step back from the bickering students. "Uh . . . is everything all right?" I asked.

"Everything's just great," Tristan said, rounding on me. "If getting a day's detention for calling Mr. Edge a moron is all right."

I cringed. "Whoa! To his face?"

Tristan shook his head. "No, I said if he thinks one day was enough to finish our assignment, then Mr. Edge is a moron." He jutted a thumb toward Jacob. "I told *him* that." He glared at his friend. "And *somehow* Mr. Edge found out about the moron part."

"Maybe someone else heard you say it," Jacob said. "You know I wouldn't do that to you."

The elevator door opened on the second floor and Tristan wheeled himself out. "Whatever," he mumbled.

Jacob ran out after him and the doors closed behind them. I was once again alone in the elevator.

Okay, that was weird, I thought. Just a little academy drama to make my elevator ride a bit more interesting, I guess.

19

I got out on the third floor and padded down the empty corridor. When I reached physics, I gently turned the handle and eased the door open. I was hoping to sneak into class without anyone making a big deal about my tumble. Luckily, all was quiet as Mrs. Lee scribbled out some formulas and figures on the digital board at the front of the classroom. She was notorious for calling out tardy students. She would often put them on the spot in a physics sort of way, asking things like how long it should've taken to get to class, calculating the distance from the restroom against the average speed of someone not wanting to be late, taking into account what kind of shoes they were wearing and things like that.

Fortunately, she continued to scribble on the board and I slinked in. The bun on the top of her head bounced up and down as she excitedly completed the work. So far, neither she nor anybody else saw me enter the classroom. If I was lucky, I'd be able to make it to my desk without anyone noticing.

I wasn't so lucky.

Mrs. Lee spun around and caught my eye. "Ah! And there's the man of the hour," she announced. She put her stylus down and began to clap. The rest of the students turned and joined her when they spotted me. Even my three friends added to the applause. Amy clapped tentatively, Sam shook her head and clapped, while Noah threw in a couple of whistles for good measure.

So much for sneaking back to class.

"Well, Tom, we were just using your latest adventure as a physics example," said Mrs. Lee.

Oh boy. Of course she was.

She turned back to the board. "We have the dimensions of the steps, their angle of descent, and Mr. Swift's weight." She turned and looked at me over her glasses. "Just a guess, mind you; there's no need to confirm or deny the figure." She nodded at the board. "Now, using these formulas, I want average velocity, and run time."

I shook my head and took my seat, but I didn't really mind that Mrs. Lee used my experiment as an example. Teachers at the academy were always coming up with new ways to teach students or using real-life events to make things more relatable. Besides, I knew I was going to get grief for it from many of the students anyway. And honestly, it was kind of a perfect example for physics class.

"Are you all right?" Sam asked as I settled into my desk.

I waved her away. "I'm fine."

She leaned closer. "You sure?"

"Oh, yeah," I replied.

"Good," she said, before punching me in the shoulder.

Amy covered her mouth in shock. Noah covered his mouth to keep from laughing.

I caught myself before shouting out. "*Hey*," I protested in a whisper. "You knew what was up. You were on crowd control."

She glanced around. Mrs. Lee was on the other side of the classroom helping a student. "I didn't know you were going to tumble down all three flights of stairs."

"At least he didn't make it to the basement," Noah said. Sam shot him a glare and Noah shrugged. "What?"

"Thanks for getting Ms. Ramos," I told Amy.

Amy kneaded her hands together. "You aren't mad?"

I shook my head. "No, it was a good idea."

Amy let out a breath and smiled.

Noah leaned over to Sam. "You know Tom was going to name his full-body airbag suit the Body Bag, right?"

Sam laughed. "No way. That's, like, the worst name ever."

"Uh, yeah," Noah said with a grin. "That's why I talked him out of it."

Jim Mills turned in his desk in front of me. "Hey, Swift. Your dad owns the company," he said. "You don't have to show off with a flashy intern project."

At fourteen, Jim was one of the older kids in the class. But he had a couple of feet on most of the students in the academy, so he seemed much older.

"Yeah, man," Jim's friend, Jason Hammond, agreed. "You don't have to make us all look bad. We all want a fair shot at an internship."

My dad's company offers summer internships to a handful of academy students at the end of every school year, and the kids with the coolest inventions usually get chosen. Jim and Jason must've thought my airbag suit was my intern project.

"Tom doesn't need a summer internship," Sam told them.

"Yeah, and if you get an internship, you'll probably have to work for my boy here," Noah added.

I shot Noah a look. "That's . . . not true at all."

I shook my head. It's not always easy being a regular student at the academy, not when your name is on the school *and* the tech company next door. Most of the time, I did a pretty good job, if I do say so myself. I didn't ask for or expect special treatment from the faculty, and I certainly didn't run to my dad anytime I had a complaint about the school. If I did that, I imagine half the students would resent me, and the other half would come to me for special privileges.

Not that my quest for normalcy mattered to my best friend. I gave Noah another harsh look. He enjoyed pushing my buttons as far as that was concerned.

"What's your intern project?" I asked Jim, trying to change the subject.

Jim opened his mouth to reply but then caught himself. He slowly shook his head. "I'm not sayin'."

Sam rolled her eyes. "No one wants to steal your project, Jim."

"Maybe not," he said with a shrug. "But you can't be too careful."

Not everyone at the academy field-tested inventions in front of the whole school. Some kept their projects a secret, but usually it was because they wanted them to be a surprise. I could only think of one instance where a student stole a project from another. And Amy is still not happy about that one.

"How are those formulas going over there, gang?" Mrs. Lee asked.

Everyone in our immediate area turned back to his or her work. I was behind. Since I was late for class, I hadn't even copied Mrs. Lee's work on the board. I pulled out a notebook and began to jot them down, but when my eyes toggled from the board back down to my paper, something caught my eye. Erin Loftice sat in a desk one row over and one row up. Like most students, her backpack was propped next to her desk, but today there was something sitting on top of it. I craned my neck to get a better look, and nearly jumped out of my seat.

It was a little plastic goblin, just like the one I had seen in Ms. Ramos's office. Its devious facial expression was the same as the one I had seen before; it looked as if it came out of the same mold. But this one seemed different somehow. Mainly because it stared at me with wide eyes and another O-shaped mouth, and this one seemed to say, "Ooh . . . look who was late to class."

I frowned at the creepy little figurine. I couldn't spin

it around, but I could ignore it. I did my best to do just that as I copied down the formulas.

Noah finished his work and turned in his desk. "Hey, did you hear that Deena and Ashley got in a big fight last period?"

"What about?" I asked.

"I don't know," Noah replied. "I just heard that they were yelling at each other."

Sam furrowed her brow. "You don't know what they said?"

Noah shrugged.

"Barely half a story." Sam shook her head. "What kind of gossip is that?"

"I just saw an argument too," I offered. I went on to tell them about my elevator ride with Tristan and Jacob.

"No way," Noah said with wide eyes. "He called him that?"

Sam nodded in approval and pointed at me. "Now that, my friends, is proper gossip."

"I like Mr. Edge," Amy said with a frown. "I don't think he's a moron."

Noah shrugged. "Sounds like he was just venting, you know?"

Sam leaned forward and squinted her eyes. "So, if Jacob didn't say anything, who did? Who would want to get Tristan in trouble? Or break up his friendship with Jacob, maybe?" Sam was sliding into her full-blown conspiracy mode.

It was cut short, however, when Mrs. Lee moved on to a few more physics formulas. Luckily, I wasn't the real-world subject of those equations.

I finished the work as quickly as I could, but I was still distracted by the creepy goblin two seats up. I didn't look at it but I could just *feel* it staring at me from its perch on the backpack. I tried to distract myself by scribbling down thoughts and ideas for lifesaving inventions. That wasn't so easy. Not only was it difficult to come up with ideas, but it was also hard to not think of the eerie little toy.

The bell rang and everyone grabbed their gear, raising the noise level in the room considerably. Because of the increased sound volume, I couldn't be 100 percent sure of what I'd heard. As I was filing out of the classroom, I heard someone say, "I want to save someone's life." It sounded just the way I had said it, but different somehow, as if whoever said it was mocking me.

I spun around to see if anyone was looking in my direction. Maybe another student had overheard me in the nurse's office and was just messing with me. I scanned the exiting crowd, but I didn't catch anyone's eye. I had no idea who had said it.

4

The Domestic Discipline

"CAN YOU EXPLAIN WHY I'M JUST HEARING about this now?" my dad asked. He paced back and forth in the dining room as he listened to a lengthy reply on his phone.

Normally, I would've playfully reminded my father that he was the one who came up with the no-phones-at-the-dinner-table rule. But tonight was different. I could tell he was very annoyed; he'd been speaking to Swift Enterprises employees from the moment he got home.

Since my mom died a few years ago, my father worked hard to be two parents in one, all while keeping business and home life separate. But sometimes when you do that *and* run a major tech company, those two worlds can't help but overlap.

The main reason I didn't give my father grief about breaking his own rule was the fact that he had yet to mention my tumble down the stairs earlier that day. I know the school called him. A student can't spend that much time in the nurse's office and not have his or her parents notified. Luckily, my father had been so preoccupied with the issue at work that he hadn't had a chance to mention my failed experiment.

"Fine," my father snapped. "But you let me know the moment you hear something." He switched off his phone and sat down at the table.

"Something wrong?" I asked, swirling my fork through my green beans.

My father shook his head. "We lost a major parts shipment last week," he replied. "Well, I say 'we,' but it was really the shipping company who *misplaced* our package." He made air quotes with his fingers when he said "misplaced." "No one in their company knows where it is, and no one in my company wanted to tell me about it for an entire week."

I kept my head down and poked at my food. He was

in a terrible mood, so this was hardly the best time to talk about my own mishap that day. On the rare occasion that I get in trouble at school, I usually try to bring it up first. My father could easily get angrier if he has to pry things out of me or if he has to broach the subject himself. In this case, though, I didn't know what to do. I just kept quiet.

Boy, was that the wrong move.

"Speaking of keeping things from me," my dad said. "You want to tell me what you were thinking when you threw yourself down a flight of stairs this afternoon?"

"It wasn't *exactly* like that," I explained. I didn't literally *throw* myself down the stairs. It was more like strategic falling. How does someone throw themselves down stairs, anyway?

My father raised an accusing eyebrow from across the table.

"Okay, it was kind of like that," I admitted. "But my airbag suit worked great."

"You went to the nurse's office," my dad said.

"Yeah, but that was just for nausea," I explained. "And so Ms. Ramos could cut me out of my suit." I went on to tell him about how my invention didn't deflate like it was supposed to.

"What if it didn't *in*flate like it was supposed to?" my father asked.

"It did, though," I said. "We had already tested it and tested it."

"But things can go wrong," he said. "Did you think about wearing a real helmet for the test? How about safety pads? Heck, how about testing it over safety mats in the gym first?"

Wow, that would've been a good idea. We could've lined up the pads on top of the bleachers and then . . .

"I'm guessing by your expression that you didn't think of any of those things," my father said.

"No," I replied, rubbing the back of my neck. "Not really. Those are really good ideas, though."

My father never told me that I should plan to fail, but he always said that I should consider all of the things that could go wrong during an experiment. Of course, you can't think of everything, but if you have contingency plans in place for as much as you can, you'll be better prepared for whatever happens. I guess I was so excited about testing my latest invention that I had forgotten that little piece of advice.

My father slowly shook his head. "What do you

think?" he asked. "Should I ground you for being so reckless?"

Boy, was that a trick question. I thought carefully before I said anything.

"Well . . . I don't know," I replied. "I *did* learn my lesson. I won't test any more dangerous inventions on myself." Then I remembered. "Oh, but I did get inspired to come up with another invention."

"Really?" my father asked. His knowing expression told me that he knew I was changing the subject.

And he was right. But I guess he didn't mind when he saw how excited I was.

I told him all about my interaction with Ms. Ramos and how she inspired me to come up with some kind of lifesaving invention.

"A noble cause." My father nodded. "Or you can come up with a first-aid technique like Henry Heimlich."

I hadn't thought of that. Dr. Heimlich invented what's now known as the Heimlich maneuver, which helps save people from choking.

"But here's a question to ask yourself: Are you doing it because you truly want to help people? Or are you doing it for praise and adulation?"

I shifted in my seat, feeling uncomfortable with the question for some reason. My father had an annoying way of turning most things into a lesson. But then again, I hadn't really thought of it that way. I guess it *would* be cool to have a Swift maneuver out there somewhere.

I shrugged. "A little of both, I guess."

"An honest answer," my father said, nodding again. "Now back to the subject of your punishment."

Darn. I sighed. "Yeah?"

My father held up three fingers. "Three flights of stairs, three full weeks of dishes and trash duties." My father and I usually traded doing the dishes and taking out the trash.

I held up a finger. "Technically, it was only two and a half flights of . . ."

My dad raised an eyebrow. "Think it should be four?"

I shook my head. "No, three is good. Three is just fine."

My father took another bite of dinner. "You know, I'd make it longer, but I get it. I pulled off some bone-headed experiments when I was your age."

"Really?" I asked. "Like what?"

My dad laughed and shook his head. "Oh, no. I'm not giving you any ideas."

5

The Incursion Diversion

I WALKED FROM THE SWIFT ENTERPRISES parking lot and across the street, toward Swift Academy. My dad and I were lucky that we had such a convenient commute. I was particularly lucky that my father had decided not to ground me as well as give me extra chores. Not that I planned on strategically falling down more stairs anytime soon. I wouldn't be forgetting about my nausea for a while.

I bounded up the steps and strolled through the main doors. But as I turned onto the first-floor hallway, I spotted the weirdest thing. Someone had attached a bunch of those creepy plastic goblins to many of the school lockers. I have to admit that I was a little weirded out by the sight—so many of those things in one place. And as I made my way to my locker, sure enough, I found one of my own staring me in the face.

"What's up with these?" asked my locker neighbor, Kevin Ryan.

"I have no idea," I replied. I plucked the figurine from my locker and turned it over to see a round magnet protruding from its back. When I turned it around, it stared up at me with the same sly expression as the others, its mouth in the same position, maniacal and stretched in that unnatural O shape.

"I wonder what these are advertising," Kevin said. He examined his own goblin as he shut his locker door.

"No idea," I said.

It wouldn't be the first time the academy had been the target of a guerilla marketing campaign. Last year, these strange stickers started appearing all over the school. They were small pairs of creepy eyes and they were stuck in the weirdest places—on bathroom stalls, in book covers, next to water fountains. I still run across a set every now and then. Those stickers turned out to be promoting a scary new VR video game called *The Witch Watcher*. Noah and I had played it, but it didn't live up to the hype.

These goblins had to be something similar. I turned the small figure over in my hands once more. It felt heavy, and had no visible seam. Whoever ran this advertising campaign spared no expense.

I turned it back around and it stared up at me once more. Then I shoved the creepy little thing into my locker and slammed the door.

"Pretty cool, huh?"

I jumped when I saw Amy standing where my locker door had been.

Amy cringed. "I didn't mean to scare you."

I let out a sigh. "That's okay." I glanced down and saw the goblin in her hand. "Oh, you got one too, huh?"

"Yeah, I wonder what they're for," she said, turning it over in her hands. "Do you think it's some kind of class project?"

I don't know if she saw the hint of revulsion on my face or my unconscious half-step backward. But either way, I could tell Amy sensed my discomfort with the figurine.

"What is it?" she asked. "It's just a toy. It's not a real goblin, you know." She grinned and pushed it toward me. I took a full step back this time.

"Cut it out," I said, beginning to get annoyed.

Amy shook her head. "I've never seen you afraid of anything," she said. "I can't believe it. *I'm* the one who's afraid of everything!"

That was true. Amy was one of the shyest people I knew. She was comfortable in our group of friends, sure. But put her with almost any other person on the planet or, heaven forbid, in front of the class to make a presentation, and she'll shut down faster than a computer going into sleep mode.

I held up both hands. "Look, I don't know what it is"—I glanced around to make sure no one else was in earshot—"but these things really creep me out."

"Really?" Amy asked. She examined her own little goblin. "I think they're cute."

"Cute?!" I exclaimed.

Amy shrugged and entered the flow of students heading for class.

I wasn't sure why the things bothered me so much. Then it hit me. I think it had something to do with a movie I saw when I was just a little kid. I don't remember much about it, only that it was full of big-eared little monsters that looked a lot like these plastic goblins. I remember having nightmares for an entire week after watching it. Now, I've seen plenty of scary movies since then. But there was just something about that one . . .

I shivered as I threw my backpack over one shoulder. I thought that making that realization would make me feel better. It did the opposite. Now I felt uneasy about the goblins *and* silly for letting some old movie get to me.

I made my way to my first class of the day, Mr. Jenkins' Algebra. My friends were already at their desks and each one of them held one of the figurines. In fact, most of the students in class had one.

"Maybe it's an alien invasion," Sam suggested. "They just *look* like harmless dolls while they're hibernating." Her eyes gleamed. "They lull us into a false sense of security before they rise up and take over the world."

"You watch *way* too much *Doctor Who*," Noah said, waving away her suggestion.

Sam raised an accusing finger. "Hey, don't diss the Doctor."

Noah raised both hands in defense. "Wouldn't dream

of it. One of my favorite shows." He nodded at me as I took my seat. "I'm thinking video game or movie promotion. What do you think?"

"I don't know," I replied as I set my pack on the floor. "And I honestly don't care," I added under my breath.

As more students filed in, many with their own goblins, Kaylee Jackson swept in with Barry Jacobs close behind. "Come on, Kaylee," Barry pleaded as they zipped by our desks. He tried to keep his voice down but it wasn't working.

"I heard you say it," Kaylee snapped at him.

"That wasn't me," Barry said.

"Just someone that sounds like you, huh?" Kaylee asked.

Their voices faded to angry murmurs as they moved to the front of the room.

Sam leaned forward in her desk. "What was that about?"

"There's been a lot of that going around lately," Amy said. "I just saw Jamal fighting with his sister in the hallway."

"And Deena and Ashley yesterday," Noah added. He nodded toward me. "Tristan and Jacob."

That was strange. I mean, sure, people get into disagreements all the time. It's human nature. But our school has always encouraged collaboration over competition. It's really weird for this many people to be at odds with each other at once.

"I heard you say it," said a voice nearby. It sounded as if it mimicked Kaylee's accusation.

Kaylee whipped around. "Who said that?"

Everyone in the classroom followed her gaze. They looked right at us.

I looked around the area. The voice sounded like it came from Amy's desk, but it wasn't her voice. Normally, Amy would be appalled by all this attention pointed just in her general direction. She would've sunk down through the floor by now. Instead, Amy held up her goblin figure and looked it over.

"I heard you say it," repeated the voice. The sound came from the goblin's O-shaped mouth, and its eyes glowed blue as it spoke. Amy nearly dropped the goblin in surprise.

It was an exact sound bite from Kaylee's previous statement. But when the goblin played it back, the speed was slightly off, so it had a mocking tone to it.

The class erupted in laughter. Amy grinned too, before she finally realized that everyone was turned toward her. Her eyes widened and she began to slump down with embarrassment, until . . .

"I heard you say it," came a voice from the front of the room.

"I heard you say it," came a voice by the door.

All around the room, goblins started repeating the phrase one after another. I felt goose bumps rise on my skin. As if these things couldn't get any creepier.

"Wow," said Noah. "These things are recorders."

Everyone in the class was examining their goblins with renewed interest. Some were shaking them, trying to get them to talk. Others were saying phrases into their ears, trying to get them to play back other things.

"I bet they're connected through the school Wi-Fi system," Sam observed as she examined her own goblin. "Or wirelessly through Bluetooth, maybe."

This really dialed up the creep factor. I could appreciate the technology, sure. But to think that these things were spying on us and then playing back sound bites through other goblins nearby . . .

And you know what? As if the freaky little thing

could read my mind, Amy's goblin played back my earlier statement.

"These things really creep me out," it said. It was in a slightly higher pitch, but you could totally tell it was my voice. Of course, if anyone hadn't figured that out, Amy certainly helped when she blurted out . . .

"That's you, Tom!"

I glared at Amy when the class erupted into laughter yet again.

To make matters worse, my words rippled throughout all the goblins in the class in different pitches and speeds, their eyes glowing as they spoke. *These things really creep me out, these things really creep me out, these things really creep me out.*

Not only was I now *extra* creeped out, I felt my face heat up as I slumped down in my seat.

The Detached Disappearance

"ALL RIGHT, PEOPLE," MR. JENKINS SAID AS HE picked up the metal trash can beside his desk and handed it to Barry Jacobs. "Those things have got to go."

The class moaned in response.

Mr. Jenkins shook his head. "I can't teach with all the jibber-jabber. I'll leave them outside and you can pick them up after class."

Everyone reluctantly dumped his or her goblin into the trash as it went by. The figures got one more laugh as several parroted Mr. Jenkins. *Jibber-jabber. Jibber-jabber.* When the can was full, Jessica Mercer set the load outside the door, and Mr. Jenkins finally began the morning's lecture.

However, he was soon interrupted again.

"Sorry for the interruption, faculty," Mr. Davenport's voice said over the intercom. Mr. Jenkins paused as everyone listened to the principal's announcement. "But it has come to my attention that our school has been invaded by a disruptive new promotion of some kind. Now, we have been over this before, but I feel I have to remind everyone that this kind of guerilla marketing on school grounds is prohibited. Therefore, I'm asking that everyone place these figurines outside of each classroom and Mr. Jacobs will come by to collect them all."

There were more grumblings from the class. Although Mr. Jenkins had promised that everyone could retrieve the goblins after class, he now shrugged and raised his hands in a *What can I do?* expression.

"I don't know who's responsible," continued the principal. "But this is a school, not a shopping mall. There will be no more of this kind of activity without repercussions. Thank you."

As Mr. Jenkins continued his lecture, I actually felt a weight leave my chest. I would never say it out loud, but knowing that those creepy things were being confiscated right outside the classroom made me feel so much better.

I shook my head at my childishness. After all, they were just stupid toys. I had way scarier action figures when I was younger.

I didn't feel so silly about being irritated at Amy. I know she didn't mean anything by it, but she should've seen that those things creeped me out. The way she waved it in my face wasn't cool at all. And to have that thing record me while she did it? You know, I do my best to help her with her anxieties and quirks, I thought she would at least return the favor.

Amy must've sensed my annoyance because she was the first one out of the class when the bell dismissed us. In fact, she seemed to avoid me the rest of the day. She and Sam didn't even join Noah and me for lunch. To be fair, we didn't always eat together. But it seemed especially convenient today. Of course, maybe I was reading too much into it—like those stupid goblins.

"I wish they didn't confiscate them all," Noah said between bites. "I would love to take one apart and see how it works."

"Good luck with that," I said sarcastically. I didn't want anything to do with it. Noah kept eating, not picking up on my tone.

After algebra had let out, we saw that Mr. Davenport had been true to his word. Mr. Jacobs, the custodian, had emptied the trash can outside. And from what we heard from other students, their goblins had also been confiscated during first period. The students were not happy. I was probably the only one who would've happily dumped one of the toys in a passing trash can.

Then I remembered why I hadn't thrown away a goblin; there was one waiting for me in my locker. Suddenly the half sandwich I had already eaten felt like a rock in my stomach.

"I know where you can get one," I told Noah, briefly explaining about how I had stashed the figurine. I sighed with relief. I could make my friend happy *and* get rid of the thing at the same time.

"Cool," Noah said with a grin. Then he raised an eyebrow. "You sure you don't want it?"

I shook my head. "No way."

Noah gave me a sly smile. "You really don't like them, do you?"

I shook my head again.

"What's up with you and those things?" he asked.

I considered telling him about my budding theory about why they freaked me out. After all, if you can't tell your best friend this kind of stuff, who can you tell? Then again, I wasn't ready for any ribbing I might get from him. That was also something best friends were good for.

"They're just not my thing," I finally replied.

"Okay," Noah said with a knowing look. "Whatever you say."

We finished lunch early and headed over to my locker. I dialed my combination and pulled open the lock. I stepped back and jutted a thumb at the closed locker. "It's all yours."

Noah grinned and moved forward. He cracked open the locker door and peered inside. His eyes widened and he gasped. "It's gone!"

"What?!" I swung the door open . . . and saw the little goblin figurine right where I left it.

I met its mischievous eyes and my insides went cold. The figure's mocking expression seeming to say, *Oooh, you fell for it.*

Noah broke into laughter. "I'm just messing with you, man."

I let out a breath and my lips tightened. "Not cool," I grunted.

"Ah, lighten up," Noah said as he opened his pack and pulled out a sweatshirt. He glanced around and then reached into the locker with the shirt, wrapping the goblin as if it would try to escape. Once the figure was bound tightly, he stashed it in his backpack and zipped it up. "I can have that thing start talking again before we get it back to your house," Noah said.

"My house?" I asked, trying to keep my voice from rising two octaves.

Noah nodded. "I'm going home with you today," he reminded me. "Remember? My parents are going out and they'll swing by for me later."

I had been so distracted by the goblins that I had completely forgotten that we had made plans to hang out at my place. I thought of what was now in Noah's backpack, and the thought of that thing in my house did not sit well with me at all.

"Oh, yeah," I said as nonchalantly as possible. I didn't want to give Noah more ammo than he already had.

Luckily, I didn't see any of the figurines for the rest of the day. Mr. Davenport had made good on his promise to confiscate them. Part of me hoped that the goblin in Noah's pack would start talking and he'd get it taken away as well, but I didn't have that much luck.

My dad picked us both up after school and took us home. We went straight to my room and got our homework out of the way. I had planned to show Noah my latest invention—the automatic standing desk. I had created a simple program that would sense how long the user had been sitting and then raise the desk automatically to help increase blood flow. Unfortunately, it wasn't quite ready for a big unveiling. It kept raising and lowering at completely random times. Stretching your legs is one thing, but getting a whole aerobic workout while trying to do your homework is something else. So I just kept it switched off for now. I could only take Noah's ribbing for one thing at a time, thank you very much.

As my father made dinner, Noah and I moved to the garage. Half of the space was a converted workroom, with large worktables and bright work lights hanging overhead. The room was warm, so I opened the garage door to let in some fresh air.

Noah pulled out the goblin, unwrapped it, and set it on the end of the worktable. He leaned close to it. "I don't see a seam to pry. What tool do you think we need to crack this sucker open?"

"Blowtorch?" I suggested.

Noah rolled his eyes. "Very funny."

I pulled out my sketch pad and placed it on the worktable, at the opposite end from the creepy figurine. "This is your project," I told Noah. "I'm working on my own thing." I wanted to get back to brainstorming my lifesaving invention.

He left the table and moved to the big rolling tool cabinet my dad kept on the other side of the garage. We'd both dug through those drawers many times working on school projects and other inventions.

"Well, help me with tool options and I'll leave you alone," Noah said.

I went over to help him and soon we amassed a nice collection of screwdrivers, picks, mini pry bars, and even an electric rotary saw. But when we turned back to the worktable with our handfuls of tools, the goblin was gone.

"Okay," I said, dumping the tools onto the worktable. "Quit messing around."

Noah put down his tools and ran to where the toy used to be. He scanned the ground near the bottom of the table. "I didn't touch it, man." He got down on all fours and looked under the table, but came up empty-handed.

"Can those things move?" I asked Noah. I shuddered as I briefly imagined the thing walking around my house on its own.

"I didn't think so," Noah said. "I thought it was just a solid piece of plastic."

Zero points of articulation made for a sorry action figure, but if you wanted something to simply sit on a shelf and stare at you in a spooky way, these things were perfect.

Regardless, even if the thing had wheels or stubby robot legs, we would've heard it hit the ground as it rolled off the table. And even then, we would've heard its tiny motors whirring as it escaped. Even the smallest remote-controlled cars made noise as they moved.

Noah and I stared at each other for a minute until a realization struck us simultaneously. We ran through the open garage door and down the driveway. I checked the dark street in both directions, but there was no one in sight.

"Too weird," Noah said. "Did someone follow us from school?"

I shook my head. "I don't know."

Noah hugged himself as if he had gotten a chill. "Okay, now *I'm* a little creeped out."

The Dissection Connection

I CRINGED AND LET OUT A SLIGHT MOAN AS SOON as I entered the school the next day. You guessed it; the lockers were once again covered with plastic goblins. However, before the academy students could marvel at their reappearance, Mr. Jacobs pushed his cart down the corridor, confiscating the figures before they could make it into any classrooms.

When I arrived at my locker, I was happy to see that the custodian had already been there. No goblin waited for me. I shoved my jacket inside my locker and closed the door. I jumped with a start when, once again, I saw Amy standing where my locker door was.

Amy winced. "I'm sorry, I'm sorry."

"That's all right," I said squarely. I released a long breath. "Déjà vu, I guess."

Amy hung her head and fidgeted with the strap on her backpack. "I'm sorry about yesterday, too. I didn't realize how much you didn't like those things."

"It's okay," I said, heading toward algebra. "It's silly anyway."

Amy shuffled up beside me. "Your feelings aren't silly," she said. "Those things obviously bug you. I shouldn't have teased you like that."

We passed Mr. Jacobs as he started on his second trash bag of goblin figurines.

"At least I don't have to worry about them anymore," I said, nodding at the custodian.

"I wish I knew what they were for," Amy said. "I bet we'll never know now."

I was fine with not knowing. If it were anything else, as someone who loves science and the pursuit of knowledge, I would be all for uncovering this mystery. But honestly, if these things were just promoting some movie, I probably wouldn't want to go see it anyway.

We got to class and I slid into my seat without another word. It felt a little weird, being annoyed with Amy, but I still felt hurt at the same time. I shook my head in disgust. I really needed to pull myself together and get over it. Friends make mistakes sometimes. I know that I've made plenty. I could tell that Amy felt bad, and now I felt as if I was just torturing her by staying annoyed with her.

I turned in my desk to talk to her when Sam and Noah swept into the room. Sam took her seat behind me while Noah plopped down at the desk beside me.

"Noah told me about what happened last night," Sam said.

"What happened?" asked Amy.

Keeping my voice low, I gave her the short version of how the goblin somehow walked away from the garage table.

"Someone took it from your house?" Amy asked.

I nodded. "I know, right?"

"And they never got to crack it open," Sam added.

Noah brought his backpack to his chest. "Thanks to Sam, that changes today." He unzipped the pack, revealing Sam's purple lunch bag inside.

I raised an eyebrow. "So you're carrying Sam's lunch for her?"

"No," said Noah. "I'm holding one of those things inside Sam's lunch bag."

I did my best to not be repulsed by the thing, even though I couldn't see it. So instead of making a face, I merely shrugged. "Okay, that makes more sense."

Sam gave me a playful shove on my shoulder. "Look, Swift. Those things communicate with each other somehow, right?"

"Yeah?" I asked.

"So my lunch bag is lined with foil," she explained. "To reflect the temperature and keep things warm or cool."

"And that foil will block any communication signals," Amy deduced. "In or out."

Using the lunch bag was a brilliant idea. I remember when Noah once put his phone in a similar lunch bag, and the battery drained because it was constantly searching for a cell signal. That's also why phones go through their batteries faster when we're stuck in a place with zero coverage.

"And that should keep it quiet until I get a chance to dissect it during lunch," Noah said with a devious grin.

It would seem that my disinterest in the goblins hadn't spread to my best friends. Everyone seemed eager to take one of those things apart and see how they worked. And if I was going to be completely honest with myself, my interest was piqued now, too. Maybe I was getting used to seeing them everywhere so they weren't *as* creepy. Or maybe just the thought of taking one apart made them less of a threat somehow. Either way, it seemed as if my fear was taking a backseat to my scientific curiosity.

Sam's plan turned out to be a solid one. The goblin tucked away in her bag didn't make a peep all through-out first period. Of course, with all of its creepy friends rounded up and piled who knows where, there wasn't really anything for the toys to spy on.

I didn't share every morning class with Noah, but when the four of us met again for lunch, he reported that the captured goblin had been silent all morning. We rushed through our lunches (Sam's now lukewarm from being in her backpack all day) and headed up to robotics class.

Luckily, the classroom was deserted. As we hoped, Mrs. Scott was probably eating her lunch in the teachers' lounge. Noah set his pack onto a worktable and began to unwrap the specimen. Meanwhile, Sam, Amy, and I sorted through Mrs. Scott's tool collection for different dissecting implements. Once we had a wide assortment, we joined Noah at the worktable. We encircled the little goblin.

I felt a little better with my three best friends backing me up. The goblin's expression even seemed less devious. It now seemed to say, *Oooh, let's talk about this, guys.*

Amy picked up the toy and turned it over in her hands. "There's no seam at all."

"That's what we found out," said Noah. "Or it's such a good, tight seal that you can't see it."

Sam raised a hacksaw and her eyes gleamed. "Then let's make our own seam."

Amy pointed to the magnet on the goblin's back. The shiny round disk was about the size of a nickel. It sat in a recessed circle in the plastic. "Maybe there's a screw behind the magnet," she said, reaching for a small screwdriver.

"Good idea," Noah said.

Sam gave a disappointed sigh as she set down her hacksaw.

Amy placed the goblin facedown and poked the tip of the standard screwdriver into the edge of the magnet's recessed circle. She gave it a twist and the magnet shifted.

"I don't think it's glued down," she said.

Amy twisted the bladed tip once more and then slid it under the magnet. She pried the metallic disk up and it popped off of the toy. It rattled across the workbench before spinning to a stop.

"Aw, there's no screw," Noah said, pointing to the empty recessed circle.

Sam picked up the hacksaw with renewed vigor. "Okay, my turn." She grabbed the goblin with her other hand, but when she lifted the toy, it split in half. The back lifted away in her hand.

"The magnet held the two halves together," Amy said as she pointed to another magnet mounted inside the other half of the toy.

Sam looked disappointed as she held the saw in one hand and half a goblin in the other.

"I'm sure we can find something else around here for you to saw open," I told her.

Sam rolled her eyes.

"Check it out," Amy said as she leaned closer to the open toy.

The interior components of the goblin were neatly laid out for all to see. A thin circuit board ran through the figure's torso. Wires led away from the board toward other components.

"Wow," said Noah. "This is one complex circuit board." He picked up a pair of tweezers and began pointing to components mounted on the board. "That's a Wi-Fi antenna, memory chip, a GPS tag, I think." He shook his head. "All this is way too expensive for a promotional giveaway."

Amy used her screwdriver to trace a wire from the circuit board to the goblin's mouth. "There's a little speaker . . ." She traced another wire to one of its ears. "That's a microphone," she said. "One in each ear."

Noah took the tweezers and tugged at another wire leading away from the circuit board. Two small devices pulled away from inside one of the goblin's eyes. One was clearly a tiny light bulb while the other . . .

"Woah," Noah whispered.

"Is that a camera?" Sam asked.

"Yeah," Noah replied. "It is."

Amy gasped. "These things are watching us, too?"

Noah poked around at the circuit board some more. He landed on two small batteries. "I don't think these have enough power to transmit video in real time. But I bet video can be uploaded later."

"Uploaded to what?" asked Sam.

Noah shrugged.

I pulled out my phone and did a quick Internet search for videos about the Swift Academy. Tons of academy students upload videos showing new inventions, experiments, or just funny things to get views, likes, and subscribers. Noah and I even have a few videos online showing some of our tests.

I scrolled through a bunch of thumbnails, many of which I recognized. I laughed when I saw a bunch of images showing me in my airbag suit, mid-tumble down the stairs. I'd forgotten that a bunch of students were recording my live-action test. I would have to go back and watch them later.

I paused on a thumbnail that showed a girl sitting in class. The image was askew, as if the video was filmed at a strange angle. The video was titled "Swift Academy Spybots: Part One." I clicked on the video and realized it was just what I was looking for.

"Check it out," I said, angling my phone so everyone could see.

The video first showed Melissa Reeves sitting in biology class. The camera angle shook as she looked directly into the lens. "Let me see that thing," she said, reaching toward the camera. Her hands seemed to grab the camera as the view spun around to show Evan Whittman sitting across from her. "You didn't get one?" he asked before the clip cut to a different location completely.

The new view showed a low angle in the gym. A group of fencers practiced in the background while a pair of sneakers walked through in the foreground.

The view changed again to show Mr. Jacobs slowly pushing his cart down the corridor. He pulled goblins off lockers and placed them into a trash bag hanging from his cart. As he neared the camera, his hand reached for it, covering the lens completely.

The view changed again, but my attention moved to the progress bar underneath the video. "Uh, there are fifty more minutes left in this video," I said.

Noah reached in and scrolled down the page. Spybot

part two was next, followed by part three and part four ...
"And at least ten more videos like this one," he said as video
after video scrolled up the screen.

I looked down at the creepy little figure. "These
things have been recording everything," I murmured.

8

The Violation
Revelation

SCIENCE TEACHES US THAT ONE CAN LEARN from failure. If an experiment doesn't go as planned, what did you learn? If an invention doesn't work the way you thought it would, how can you build it differently? Well, after a couple of mishaps in the past, where my friends and I tried to solve mysteries by ourselves, I did learn one important thing: Sometimes it's best to just tell someone in authority right away.

"We should tell Mr. Davenport," I suggested. "It doesn't matter if this is a movie promotion or . . ."

"Or some other school, looking for our secrets," Sam

suggested. Her eyes widened. "Or maybe it's some other country."

Sam was always big on conspiracy theories. Normally, I would've been right there with her, brainstorming all the different possibilities, all the possible adversaries. But to me, obviously, these . . . spybots were no laughing matter.

"Whoever made them," I said, "we should report what we know right now."

"Wow, Swift," Sam said, eyeing me suspiciously. "These things must really bug you."

Amy kneaded her hands together but didn't add anything.

"Yeah, man," said Noah. "Because I bet I can hack into this one and learn more about . . ."

"That's fine and all," I said with a nod. "But there are some major privacy issues here. We have to tell Davenport before another batch appears."

I turned to leave, but Sam caught my arm. "Wait, won't we get in trouble for not turning this one in?"

"I hadn't thought of that," I said.

Mr. Davenport had seemed pretty annoyed during his announcements. He might not like the fact that some of his students didn't hand over one of the banned toys. But then again, this was the Swift Academy of Science and Technology. How upset could he be at a few of the students wanting to take one of the things apart to see how it worked?

Noah raised both hands. "Wait a minute. Let's say, for the sake of argument, that we do turn this one in." He shrugged. "Just . . . not right now."

"What?" Amy asked.

"If I have a little more time with this one," Noah explained, "I might be able to tap into some of the other spybots and see what they see."

Amy covered her mouth. "You want to spy on people?"

"No, no," Noah replied. "I mean . . . yeah." He raised a finger. "But only whoever created these. We could find out who they are. Besides, who else *could* we spy on? All the other ones were confiscated."

"Oh," Amy said.

Sam grinned. "Davenport doesn't have to know we cracked one open. Just that we found the videos."

"Okay," I agreed. I guess half of my come-clean plan was better than none at all. I had to admit that I, too, was curious about who created these creepy things. And if there was a way to get rid of the toys once and for all, then I was all for it.

Amy put the spybot back together and Noah shoved it into Sam's lunch bag. Then he tucked it into one of the cubbyholes Mrs. Scott had for her students. Noah, Sam, and I had robotics that afternoon, so he could work on it some more then.

We still had some time left in our lunch period, so the four of us marched downstairs toward the principal's office.

Ms. Lane, the office manager, wasn't at her desk, but we caught Mr. Davenport in his office. I knocked on the open door as I leaned in.

"Mr. Swift," the principal said. Then as the rest of the group stepped in. "Miss Watson, Miss Hsu, Mr. Newton. What are we confessing to this time?" His eyes fell on Amy.

The last time the four of us went to the principal's office, we were backing up Amy as she confessed about creating an app that helped predict pop quizzes.

Amy stared at her feet in response to his gaze.

"Nothing," I quickly jumped in. "We just wanted to tell you about what we learned about those goblin things."

The principal's eyes widened. "Do you know who brought them?"

I shook my head. "No, but we found out something you're not going to like."

I told him about the online videos and dug out my phone to show him. While I continued the video we started earlier, Noah, Sam, and Amy pulled out their phones and pulled up other videos.

Mr. Davenport shook his head as his eyes bounced from each of our outstretched screens. Four montages played at once, showing academy students in locations all over the school. "This is not good," he said. "Not good at all. These were all filmed without consent. These are huge privacy violations."

As he continued to stare in amazement, I heard a familiar voice coming from one of the phones. It was Amy's voice saying, "It's just a toy. It's not a real goblin, you know." My eyes widened as I looked at the screen on Amy's phone and saw myself looking directly into camera. The distorted, close-up shot of my face showed equal parts fear and disgust as I backed away.

Realizing what was playing, Amy gasped. With

fumbling fingers, she stopped the video and slid the phone into her pocket.

My lips tightened and I felt my face flush with embarrassment. My scared face was all over the Internet for anyone to see. Here I was, thinking I had put my fears aside while we learned more about these creepy goblins. Instead, I literally came face-to-face with the kid from yesterday who seemed repulsed and terrified of a stupid little toy.

A fresh wave of annoyance washed over me as I glared at Amy.

But Mr. Davenport didn't notice. He stared at the three remaining screens a little longer before finally waving them away. "All right, I've seen enough."

"Who would do this?" Sam asked.

Mr. Davenport shook his head. "I wish I knew."

"Doesn't the school have surveillance?" asked Noah. "So you can see who dropped them off?"

"You're a smart kid, Mr. Newton," Davenport said. "But we already thought of that." He got to his feet. "Trouble is, the surveillance system has been offline for the past few days."

We moved out of the way as he stepped around his

desk, heading for the office door. He motioned for us to follow. "The great thing about this school, though, is that there is no shortage of tech support volunteers."

We followed the principal into the small hallway. From the corner of my eye, I saw Amy give me a couple of nervous glances. I ignored her, and kept my eyes on Davenport.

Our principal opened the door to the room next to his office. Dim light shone from two large computer monitors showing streaming lines and lines of code. Jim Mills, from my physics class, sat at the desk, typing on a keyboard. He looked up as we entered.

"Any luck, Mr. Mills?" asked Mr. Davenport.

"No, sir," Jim replied. "I think there's a corrupted file somewhere in the system. I'm going to reinstall the entire software package."

The principal raised both hands in a *There you go* sort of gesture.

"I can help go through the code, if you like," Noah offered.

Jim shook his head. "I think a reinstall will be faster, but thanks."

Mr. Davenport backed out of the office, closing the

door behind him. "Thanks for showing me the videos," he said. "I better work on my form letter response to all the angry parent e-mails that I'm sure I'll get by morning."

The four of us left the office and headed out into the main hallway.

"Tom?" Amy said.

"Not now, Amy," I snapped.

"But I just want to . . ."

"I don't want to hear it," I said, quickening my pace.

I really didn't want to go off on her, but I couldn't trust myself not to, the way I felt at that very moment. I was humiliated all over again, but this time on a whole new scale. Now, the rest of the school, heck, the rest of the *world*, could see me scared of some stupid little toy. I put some space between us as I stormed down the hall. If I didn't get away from her, there was no telling what I would say.

"Amy isn't the one to blame, you know," Noah said as he caught up to me. "You should really be angry at whoever built those spybots."

I sighed and shook my head. "Whatever."

Even though I was annoyed with Amy, and now with Noah for standing up for her, I had to admit that I was mostly mad at myself for having such an irrational fear of some stupid little goblin character in the first place. I couldn't even be mad at the builders for choosing the one creature that would freak me out. I just wish I knew why they bugged me so much. I get that I was just a little kid when that movie scared me. But now that I'm older, with a more logical mind, it really shouldn't bother me so much. Should it?

"Hey, man." Noah grabbed my arm. "Don't worry. I'll hack that thing and we'll find a way to figure out who's behind it all."

I shrugged him off and opened my mouth to reply. After a moment, I let out a long breath and rubbed the back of my neck. "I guess so," I finally said.

"See?" Noah grinned. "It's always nice having a goal to work toward, keeping your mind occupied."

That was a good point. I pushed the goblins and the embarrassing video out of my mind. I tried to focus on my new invention. Or, better yet, on finding out who was behind the toys in the first place.

A smile pulled at my lips. "I bet they're worried that we're onto them, too."

"What do you mean?" asked Noah.

"The new video we just made," I explained. "You know there's probably one of the four of us, surrounding that thing, trying to figure out how to take it apart."

"Oh, yeah!" Noah laughed. "And what about when I pulled that camera out of the eyehole. I bet it looked freaky, whipping around the robotics classroom. . . ." His grin disappeared.

The same thought hit me at the same time. If the spybot creator saw the video of us in the robotics classroom, he or she knows exactly where it is. It didn't matter that the GPS tag or Wi-Fi antenna were blocked while it was in the lunch bag. They were certainly active while we were examining it.

Without another word, Noah and I sprinted toward the stairs. We flew up the steps two at a time, dodging and sidestepping other students along the way. We hit the third-floor landing and Noah pulled ahead. He zipped into the robotics classroom just before me. By the time I made it inside, I saw Noah standing by the cubbies, holding Sam's empty lunch sack.

The Unproductive
Deduction

"STUPID, STUPID, STUPID," NOAH SAID, SHAKING his head. He shoved the empty bag back into the cubby. "I should've held on to it the entire time."

For the first time, I wasn't happy to see one of those goblins disappear. We'd actually had a shot at finding out who was behind those things, and now that shot was gone.

"I'll ask around," Noah said. "Can you think of anyone else who stashed one?"

I shook my head. "I have no idea."

I tried to think back to everyone who had actually

enjoyed those things, especially at the beginning when everyone pulled them off their lockers and carried them around. And knowing the kind of students at the academy, we probably weren't the first ones to try to take one apart. I wonder if any of those curious students had their goblin mysteriously vanish like ours.

Then I remembered the very first time I had seen a goblin.

"Wait a minute," I told him. "I think I might know where one is."

I told Noah about my time in Ms. Ramos's office and the goblin I spotted there.

"But that was like a whole day before everyone else had one," Noah pointed out. "Are you sure it was the same thing?"

"Oh yeah," I said. "And remember when I told you how I wanted to invent something to save lives?"

"Yeah?" Noah asked.

"Well, I first got the idea in her office," I explained. "And then the next day, in algebra class, when a bunch of people had those goblins, I thought I heard someone making fun of me. Saying exactly what I had said in the nurse's office."

Noah's eyes widened. "That thing recorded you!"

"I think so," I agreed. "And another one played back my words later in algebra class."

"Sheesh," Noah said, rubbing his head. "No wonder they creep you out."

"Right?" I said.

"So . . ." Noah raised an eyebrow. "Do you think she still has it?"

"I don't know." I shrugged. "She's not a student, so maybe she didn't have to turn it in. And I can't see the creator being brave enough to swipe it out of her office. Either way, I'll find out."

I didn't have time to stop by her office before lunch period was over, so Noah and I split up, heading out to class, business as usual.

I tried to concentrate on Mrs. Gaines's lecture as I sat through chemistry class. But I did find myself scoping out the other students' backpacks, wondering if any of them had stashed one before this last invasion was confiscated.

When the bell rang, I was the first person out the door. I moved through the flow of students and headed for the stairs. I ran down to the first floor (much better than tumbling) and made my way to the nurse's office.

I knocked on the open door and stepped inside. "Ms. Ramos?"

She wasn't there.

I moved toward her desk. I spotted the photos of her kids, but I didn't see the goblin. I crouched down to see if it had fallen to the floor. I half expected it to be staring back at me as it hid behind dust bunnies and computer cables.

"Tom?"

"Ah!" I blurted out as I stood and spun around.

Ms. Ramos stood in the doorway with a concerned look on her face. "Is everything all right?"

I caught my breath. "It's fine. I mean—I'm fine," I stammered.

She crossed her arms. "Well, what can I do for you?"

"You see, when I was here the other day, I saw that you had one of those goblin things." I pointed to her desk.

Ms. Ramos nodded and smiled. "Yes, it was a gift from one of my patients."

I rubbed the back of my neck. "Well, I was wondering if I could borrow it for a while."

The nurse sat behind her desk. "I'm afraid you'll have to ask Mr. Davenport," she said. "I turned it in to him when he confiscated the rest of them."

My shoulders dropped. "Oh."

She leaned forward. "Did you know that those things recorded what people said?"

I gave a half smile. "I had heard that, yeah."

Ms. Ramos shook her head. "We can't have that in a nurse's office, can we?"

"I guess not," I said as I moved toward the door. Before I stepped out, a thought occurred to me. I spun around. "Who gave it to you?"

Ms. Ramos smiled. "I can't tell you that. It was one of my patients." She leaned back in her chair. "I'm not necessarily claiming doctor-patient confidentiality, but you wouldn't like it if I told another student that you were a patient of mine the other day, would you?"

I rolled my eyes. "I think half the school saw me waddling down the hall and into your office."

Ms. Ramos's hand shot to her mouth as she stifled a laugh. "Fair enough. But if they *hadn't* seen you come in here, it wouldn't be right to share that information with anyone, would it?"

I shrugged. "I guess not. Thanks anyway."

I had just enough time to make it back up to the third floor for robotics class. I joined Sam and Noah at our worktable and told them how I had struck out.

"Aw, man," Noah said.

"So Ms. Ramos is not saying who gave it to her?" Sam asked.

I shook my head. "There's really no guarantee that whoever gave her the goblin created these things," I said. "Her patient could've been one of the first people to get one and just didn't like it, like me."

Sam poked my chest. "Speaking of, you need to ease up on Amy. She feels horrible about embarrassing you like that. It's not her fault those things recorded you."

"First of all . . . *ow!*" I said as I rubbed my chest. "And second of all . . ." I let out a sigh. "I know. She just wouldn't ease up on me. And now my reaction is all over the Internet."

"Why do you hate those things so much?" Sam asked.

I thought of telling her about the movie that frightened me when I was little, but it just seemed too silly to say out loud. Instead, I simply sighed and shook my head. "I don't want to talk about it."

Luckily, Sam didn't push it and we didn't talk about anything to do with spybots for the rest of the class.

We continued working on Mrs. Scott's latest project—building a robotic arm that can play checkers in real time. Noah and Jamal Watts had created the software while the rest of the class worked on arms with the dexterity to handle the little plastic checker pieces. Little-known fact: The hardest part was getting it to properly king the opposing player.

When class was dismissed, the three of us were surprised to find Amy waiting outside the classroom. She didn't say a word, but motioned us over to the side, out of the flow of traffic. After we joined her, she looked down and unzipped her backpack, revealing a spybot staring back up at us.

"Way to go, Ames!" said Noah.

The Position
Transmission

"TONY NGUYEN GAVE IT TO ME DURING FENCING
practice," Amy said. "He hid one before they were confiscated this morning, but then worried he was going to
get in trouble." She glanced around. "Now I know how
he feels."

"Don't worry, I'm on it." Noah snatched the backpack
and ran back into the classroom.

"Where can we take it apart now?" Sam asked.

"Why don't we meet at my house?" I suggested. "My
dad can give us a ride after school."

"Cool," Sam agreed.

It wasn't unusual for the four of us to work on projects in my dad's garage. Of course, it was a bit unusual for us to work on a project that would possibly unmask someone who wanted to spy on all the Swift Academy students. Either way, I didn't think my dad would mind the last-minute company.

Amy looked down. "All of us?"

I sighed. "Yes, all of us, Amy."

Sam gave me a nudge.

"What?" I asked her.

Noah ran back out of the classroom and handed Amy her backpack. Noah held up Sam's purple lunch bag in the other hand. "I'm not letting this thing out of my sight now."

I told him our plan as he slid the lunch bag into his backpack, and we all went off to our next class. Now that the foil blocked the audio, video, and GPS transmissions, there was no way for anyone to track the goblin's location.

After school, as predicted, my father was fine with shuttling us back to our house.

"Big project, huh?" he asked as we piled into the car.

"Oh, yeah," Noah replied.

My dad caught my eye in the rearview mirror as he

pulled away. "Does this have anything to do with your lifesaving invention?"

"Uh . . ." For some reason, the question threw me for a second. "Not really."

"Why don't you tell me about it over pizza?" he said.

My friends and I eyed each other nervously. Were we ready to explain everything to my dad yet? Would he be upset that we held on to something that Mr. Davenport had confiscated?

Before any of us could say anything, my father's phone rang. He put a finger to his lips, telling us to keep quiet, before he pressed a button on the steering wheel.

"Tell me you have good news, Bryce," he said.

"Uh, yes and no," replied a voice from the car's speakers. It was my father's assistant.

My dad's brow furrowed. "What does that mean?"

"Okay, the shipment definitely made it to Shopton," Bryce replied.

"And . . . ," said my dad.

Bryce sighed. "And . . . that's all anyone knows."

"So, it's in town," said my dad. "Which is something, but it's still missing."

"Essentially, sir," Bryce replied.

My father sighed in disappointment.

I quietly filled my friends in on Swift Enterprises's missing shipment as my dad made two more calls on the way home. Luckily for us, he had completely forgotten about our project.

When we got home, he disappeared into his home office and we headed for the garage. Soon, the four of us surrounded Sam's lunch bag as it sat on the worktable.

"Okay," said Noah. "As soon as we open this thing, it will begin transmitting."

"Can we pull out the batteries?" Amy asked.

Noah nodded. "We could, but I need the motherboard powered when I hook it up to my laptop."

"We could disconnect the cameras and microphones," I suggested.

"I like that," Noah said. "I could just snip the wires."

"What about the GPS tag?" Sam asked.

Noah shook his head. "It's soldered onto the motherboard. No way to remove that without damaging it."

"So as soon as we open that bag, they'll know exactly where it is?" Amy asked.

"Yeah, but after I snip the wires to the cameras and

microphones, they won't know what we're doing with it," Noah replied.

Sam got that gleam in her eye. You know … the scary hacksaw gleam. "Okay, let's do it."

"All right," Noah said, taking the lead. "But let's get everything ready before we open the bag."

While Noah readied his laptop, the rest of us grabbed whatever tools we thought we might need.

Once everything was set, Noah reached for the bag. "Okay, no one say a word."

Noah opened the bag and pulled out the spybot as quickly as possible. He flipped it onto its front while Amy reached in with a screwdriver. She popped off the magnet and Sam pulled off the back. As soon as the circuit board was exposed, I handed a pair of nippers to Noah and he snipped the wires leading from one eye and one ear. I swiftly did the same with my own pair of nippers.

Once the operation was complete, everyone seemed to let out a sigh.

"Now what?" asked Amy.

Noah hunched over the disabled spybot. "Now, I work my magic." He clamped two small alligator clips onto parts of the motherboard. The clipped wires led back to an exposed circuit board jutting out of a USB port on his laptop. From the look of it, I could tell it was an interface Noah had rigged up just for the occasion.

I pushed back from the worktable and paced the floor. Now it was all on Noah. My best friend typed away as he worked to interface his laptop with the spybot.

"How long is this going to take?" Sam asked.

"I don't know," Noah replied.

"Hey, gang," my dad said as he entered the garage. "The pizza should be here in about fifteen . . ." His voice trailed off when he saw what must've been a weird scene. Wires trailed from Noah's laptop to a dissected toy. He cocked his head. "What are you doing?"

There was no escaping it. With everything laid out on the worktable for all to see, we had to tell my dad the whole story now. I just hoped he would understand why we didn't turn in this particular spybot.

I let out a long breath. "So . . . these . . . toys begin appearing at our school . . ."

"And they record what people say, and play it back," Sam continued.

"But they're all connected," I added. "And we just found out that they record video and upload them to . . ."

My dad stepped closer, staring at the open goblin. He didn't seem to be listening as he slowly raised a finger and pointed at the circuit board. "Where did you get that?"

I frowned. "That's what I was saying. These things just started appearing at our school a few days ago."

Sam, Amy, and I told my dad the whole story all over again. Noah added a detail now and then, but he mostly kept working on his computer.

When we were done, my dad leaned over the open spybot once more. "And you say Davenport had them all confiscated?"

I cringed and jutted a thumb at the one on the table. "Well, *most* of them."

"Do you think he destroyed them?" my father asked. He didn't seem to care that we held one back.

"We don't know," Sam replied. "Mr. Jacobs collected them."

"I have to call Mr. Davenport right now," my dad said as he spun on his heel and headed toward the door.

"Why?" I asked.

My father stopped and raised an accusing finger at the open spybot. "Because that circuit board right there? *That's* part of my missing shipment." He disappeared back into the house.

The four of us glanced at each other with wide eyes.

"So, someone *stole* Swift Enterprises tech and put it into a bunch of . . . toys?" Sam asked. "That doesn't make any sense."

"It does seem a little overkill, if you ask me," Noah chimed in as he continued typing.

"What do you mean?" asked Amy.

Noah pointed at the open goblin. "This circuitry is way too sophisticated for a movie promo, or even an expensive toy. There's stuff on this board that I haven't even identified yet."

Sam crossed her arms and nodded. "I'm totally revisiting my theory about a foreign government spying on us."

What really gnawed at the back of my mind was the fact that my father's company would have a circuit board like that in the first place. I know that Swift Enterprises is a big government contractor and they work on all kinds of top-secret projects, but would they really be involved with a project that spies on people like that?

"Okay, I'm in," Noah announced.

We gathered around him and stared at a black computer screen. A few red dots broke up the blackness.

"I was able to ping a signal off the other spybots," Noah explained. He pointed to a red dot in the center of the screen. "This is the one here, in the garage." Noah widened to show two more nearby dots and then a big cluster of them. "And here are all the others."

"Can you add a city map overlay?" Amy asked.

"Already working on it," Noah said as his fingers blurred across the keyboard.

Soon a map of Shopton appeared on the screen. I recognized my street immediately, and the red dot in the center sat right were my house would be. Noah widened to include the nearby dots.

"Those must be other students who snuck goblins home," Sam said, pointing to the other dots.

"That's what I was thinking," said Noah.

"Go to that big cluster," I suggested. I had a pretty good idea where they would fall on the map.

Noah moved the map until dozens of red blips clumped in the center of the screen. Sure enough, those dots were in the center of the academy.

"Those are all the ones Mr. Davenport confiscated," Amy said.

I nodded. "At least we can tell my dad that they weren't destroyed."

"Widen out again," Sam instructed.

Noah did just that and we saw a wider view of Shopton. Again, there was only our dot, two more in other neighborhoods, and the cluster at the school.

Amy pointed at one of the outlying blips. "Do you think one of those could be with whoever created these?"

Noah shrugged. "Could be. Although they may not need to tie into a spybot to track the others like I did."

Just then, another cluster of dots appeared on the upper right section of the screen. It vanished just as quickly as it had appeared.

"Did anyone else see that?" I asked.

"Yeah," Sam replied. "Another group of them . . . just for a second."

I pointed to that part of the screen. "Can you zoom in on this section?"

Noah drew a box around the area and clicked a button. That section of Shopton enlarged to fill the screen.

It was a nearby business district full of warehouses and small supply houses. My dad had taken me to a paper company there before, to buy custom paper rolls for a model rocket project.

Everyone stared at the map in silence, but the area remained clear of dots. If Sam hadn't seen the blip as well, I would've wondered if I had been seeing things. But just as my eyes began to water from keeping them open for so long, the group of red dots appeared again.

Noah quickly enlarged the area, and the cluster spread out a little as he zoomed in. There looked like there were dozens of spybots in that area.

Amy pointed at the screen. "There!"

The dots were clustered over the large building before blinking out again. The map labeled the building as "U-Lock-Up Storage."

"Hey, I know that place," Noah said. "My grand-mother has a storage unit there."

"Why are they blinking off and on like that?" asked Sam.

I shook my head. "I have no idea."

Noah's arms shot up. "I do! That whole place is metal—the siding, the roll-up doors, everything."

"And the metal blocks the signal," Amy added.

The cluster of the lights blinked on again.

"And when someone opens the door, the signals can get out," I said.

"That's a big place," Noah said. "I don't know how we'll be able to find out which unit they're using."

I pointed to the screen and shrugged. "Maybe we can look for whoever is opening and closing a door?"

11

The Reverberating Reconnaissance

NOAH AND I PEDALED DOWN THE DARK STREET.
The storage place wasn't far away, but there was no telling when the spybot creator would lock up for the night. So I had hopped on my bike (while Noah borrowed my dad's) and we headed over as quickly as we could.

Sam and Amy decided to stay and monitor the computer, and also fill in my dad when he got off the phone. I tried to let him know the situation before we left, but he was busy contacting company employees now that the missing circuit boards had turned up. Although this was another one of my act-first-think-later plans, I didn't think my father would be too upset. Besides, this might be our only chance to find out once and for all who was behind the spybots.

We turned down another street and the storage place came into view on the left. Long, thin buildings held rows of storage units, each with a metal roll-up door and a regular entry door.

Noah took the lead as he pulled into the main entrance. He parked in front of a small keypad and shook his head. "I never thought getting dragged along to this place would come in handy." He punched in the code, the keypad beeped, and a large chain-link gate rolled to one side.

We pedaled through the entrance and down between two of the long buildings.

"Nobody's here," Noah whispered.

"There has to be," I said, pulling out my phone. I stopped my bike long enough to shoot Sam a text.

Anything? I wrote.

They haven't appeared again yet, she replied.

I hoped we weren't too late. If the spybot creator had left for the night, we'd never find out which unit they were using.

I supposed my father could go to the police to get a search warrant. But would they issue a warrant based on some kids hacking into a toy to track other toys that contained stolen technology? Heck, *I* barely believed it.

We reached the end of the long building and pedaled past the end. As we turned between the next two buildings, I received a text from Sam. **They're back**.

Up ahead, a car was parked at the far end of the building. An entry door was propped open and light poured out of the storage unit.

"Check it," I whispered to Noah.

We parked our bikes at the end of the building and crept toward the open door. I heard voices as we approached, but I couldn't make out what they were saying.

We made our way through the shadows until we reached the open door. Noah and I crouched behind the door and listened. The voices fell silent.

I glanced at Noah and he motioned for me to take a look. I pointed at my chest and mouthed, *Me?* Noah just shrugged.

I shook my head and slowly peeked around the door. I spotted a man reaching for a large plastic bin on the top shelf of a shelving unit.

"You're sure it's in this one?" the man asked.

"No, but we haven't checked it yet," replied a woman's voice.

I looked farther around the door to see a woman standing with her back to me. She had her hands out as if ready to catch the man if he fell.

I quickly scanned the rest of the space. It was full of stacked furniture, sporting equipment, and shelves of large plastic bins. There wasn't a goblin in sight.

"I still think we sold it in the garage sale," the man said, straining to pull the large bin off the shelf.

"We better not have," said the woman. "That was his favorite jacket."

I eased back into the shadows and shook my head at Noah. Whoever these people were, they weren't behind the spybots.

We silently made our way back to our bikes. Just before I climbed on, I heard a voice coming from the other side of the building. I caught Noah's eye and pointed in that direction.

We both crept to the corner and poked our heads around. A bike lay on the ground and a tall figure stood near an open door, three units down. He was facing

97

our direction, but no light shone from inside the unit, so I couldn't make out his face. He held a phone up to his ear.

"...stop? Just like that?" the figure asked. It was a male voice that sounded kind of familiar, but I couldn't place it. Plus, he was so far away that I couldn't make out everything he said. "What ... supposed to do with ..."

The fact that the mystery person had a bike there like us, and his voice sounded familiar, *and* there were tons of videos uploaded to the web, made me suspect that the culprit was an academy student like us.

Noah and I glanced at each other. This sounded more promising.

"Hello?" the person asked. "Hello ... hear me?"

He stepped all the way out of the doorway and the door shut behind him. Noah and I ducked back behind the corner as he began walking in our direction.

"Hello?" his voice asked again, much louder this time. "You're breaking up."

I held my breath as he walked closer to our hiding spot.

"... little better," the voice said, a bit quieter now.

I poked my head out to see that the figure was walking in the opposite direction now. His voice faded as he moved farther down between the two buildings.

"Come on," I whispered to Noah.

Noah and I left our hiding place and jogged down to the third doorway. Noah opened the door and stepped inside. I was about to go after him when I noticed a combination padlock on the ground. I picked it up before following Noah inside. I wanted to be long gone before the guy came back, but just in case, I didn't want to end up locked inside the unit. And after I switched on my phone's flashlight app and saw where we were, I liked the idea even less.

I gasped and my blood turned to ice as my light shone over shelves upon shelves of the spybots. If you think they looked creepy by themselves, imagine dozens and dozens of them, an entire army, all lined up as if they were ready for a full-scale invasion. They looked down at us with devious expressions, silent and waiting.

We had found the correct storage unit, all right. My heart raced, and it took all I could do to keep from running out of there.

"Whoa," Noah said.

"*Whoa-whoa-whoa-whoa,*" the goblins replied, Noah's

voice rippling through the unit. Each voice was in a different pitch and their eyes glowed as they spoke, creating an eerie light show inside the storage unit.

"Oh man," Noah said, a tremor in his voice.

"Oh man, oh man, oh man, oh man," the goblins all replied.

I covered Noah's mouth before he could say anything else. The light from my phone reflected in his terrified eyes.

"Let's get out of here," I whispered, and then immediately regretted it.

"Out of here, out of here, out of here," whispered the goblins.

We didn't need any more convincing. We ran for the door, but as soon as my hand was on the knob, I heard a voice on the other side.

"Hang on," said the person. "I can't find the lock."

My eyes widened. I turned to Noah and aimed my phone at my other hand, showing him the padlock.

Dude! Noah mouthed.

I shrugged in reply and then froze when the large roll-up door began to rattle. Whoever was behind the spybot invasion was about to open the big door and see

Noah and me standing there. I spun my light around the unit but there was nowhere to hide. We were so busted.

"Never mind," the voice said. "I'll just grab one of the locks from the big door."

A couple of the goblins replied, *"Big door, big door."*

A metallic rattle came from the other side of the door as a new padlock was attached. After that, I could swear I heard a bicycle being pedaled away.

We were trapped.

12

The Replication Liberation

"WHAT WERE YOU THINKING?" NOAH ASKED.

Then the goblins repeated the question. *"What were you thinking, thinking, thinking?"*

I held up the lock. "I was trying to keep us from getting locked in."

"Locked in, locked in," the spybots taunted.

Noah cringed at the sound.

I held up my phone. "Look, my dad has some bolt cutters. I'll call him and he'll get us out of here."

As the spybots repeated my words, Noah just shook his head. "Yeah, right. Good luck with that."

"Good luck with that, luck with that," they agreed.

As I held up my phone, I realized what Noah must've already figured out. If the spybot signals couldn't get out of the storage unit, neither could a cell signal.

I jutted a thumb at the back of the unit. "What about the couple next door?" I asked. "They might be able to hear us."

Noah ignored the repeating goblins. "And they have bolt cutters in there?"

"No, but they could call my dad," I said.

Noah shrugged. "Worth a try."

"Worth a try, worth a try," taunted the goblins as we moved to the roll-up door.

We both beat with our fists. "Help!" we shouted. "Help! We're trapped!"

The goblins joined in with our pleas. Half of them seemed to be helping us while the other half sounded as if they were mocking us. My heart seemed to beat faster with every sound they made.

We stopped and waited for the last of the spybots to finish their cycle. I breathed a little easier when they were silent again. We listened carefully, but heard nothing from the other side of the door.

Noah slid down the door and sat on the ground. "Sam and Amy know we're here," he said, hanging his head. "They'll come looking for us eventually."

"Eventually, eventually."

I shivered. Who knows how long it would take for Sam and Amy to show up? The thought of spending more time trapped with the army of goblins moved me to act. I used my phone to scan the rest of the storage unit. There had to be *something* in here besides those creepy things. There were some legitimate storage items in the unit. Some cardboard boxes, some furniture. Unfortunately, whoever rented this unit didn't need it to store an extra crowbar or two.

I shook my head and moved back toward the main door. I used my flashlight to find the light switch. I flicked it on and the unit was awash with bright fluorescent lighting.

I sighed with relief. Even though the sheer number of goblins ratcheted up their creep factor, the bright light took it back down again. Noah must've felt the same way. He blinked and then grinned.

"Cool," he said, getting to his feet.

The goblin choir agreed with him.

Noah moved to the back wall to ogle over something that I hadn't noticed yet—two big, state-of-the-art 3-D printers. He ran his hand over one of them. "These are the new Technin one hundreds," he said. "They're supposed to be crazy fast."

"*Fast, fast,*" agreed the goblins.

I looked up at the rows of creepy figures. "That's how they made so many of them."

"Tom?" came a faint voice. "Noah?"

Noah and I glanced at each other and then ran to the roll-up door and began banging again.

"In here!" I shouted.

"*In here, in here,*" repeated the goblins.

"Guys? Are you in there?" Sam asked, followed by knocking from her side.

Noah and I laughed.

"Yes, in here!" Noah shouted. The goblins mimicked him.

"Your dad brought us," Sam said. "He's going to go back and get some bolt cutters for the locks."

I remembered the lock I brought inside. "Wait a minute," I said, grabbing the lock from beside the closed door.

I checked the combination dial on the open lock. The numbers read: 2-0-0-5. That could have been someone's birth year. That would make sense if the culprit was closer to my age.

"Try two, zero, zero, five," I suggested.

"*Zero, zero, five,*" repeated the goblins.

There was a pause and then . . .

"That did it," Sam announced.

Noah and I laughed and pushed up on the metal door. It didn't budge.

"I thought you unlocked it," I said.

After the goblin chorus died down, Sam said, "Tell Amy you're not mad anymore."

"What?" I asked.

"*What, what, what,*" the goblins asked.

"Cut it out, Sam," I heard Amy say outside.

"Tell Amy you're not mad at her anymore," Sam repeated.

I sighed. I wasn't mad at Amy anymore, but I was about to be mad at Sam.

"I'm not mad anymore, Amy," I said. The goblins repeated my words.

"Is there an echo in there?" asked Sam.

"Come on!" I said.

"Come on, come on, come on."

"And tell her you're sorry for being mean to her," Sam ordered.

I shook my head. "*I* was mean?"

"Dude, do it. Just do it," Noah said, rubbing his face in frustration.

The goblins chanted their agreement. *"Do it, do it, do it, do it."*

My head dropped. "I'm not mad anymore. I'm sorry I was mean, and I'll never do it again. Can you *please* let us out now?!"

As the spybots finished their mockery of my apology, the door slid open. Sam stood there with a smug look on her face. Amy looked extremely embarrassed, while my dad frowned and shook his head.

"Uh . . . we found the rest of your circuit boards," I told him.

13

The Entrapment
Gambit

NOAH AND I LOADED THE BIKES INTO THE TRUNK
and my dad drove us home for cold pizza. To everyone's
surprise, he didn't want us to grab any of the spybots from
the storage unit. He had us lock the door and leave it just
as we had found it. Even though someone had stolen the
circuit boards from him, he said he couldn't just steal them
back. He had to get them back legally and not trespass
onto private property to do it—something Noah and I had
just done, he reminded us. It may take a while to discover
who rents the storage unit, but he would figure it out and
decide whether or not to get the police involved.

"What is your company going to do with those circuit boards?" Noah asked between bites of pizza. "Are you going to spy on your employees?"

"Oh, no," my dad replied. "Nothing like that."

"It's probably for some top-secret project," Amy said, giving Noah a stern look.

My dad shook his head. "No, not that, either."

"So you can tell us?" I asked.

"Sure," he said. "I don't have to tell you four how industrial espionage is a genuine concern at our company."

"Oh, yeah," agreed Sam.

During a recent field trip to Swift Enterprises, the four of us (along with a couple of unexpected guests) helped stop a would-be techno thief from stealing company secrets.

"Well, as you know, no recording devices are allowed past security," my dad continued. "No phones, digital recorders, thumb drives, cameras." He pointed toward the garage. "And from what you told me about those . . . spybots, if that was a real toy, you couldn't bring something like that in, either."

"Okay," I said. "But those circuit boards are made for recording."

My dad raised a finger. "Exactly. I wanted to create

a proprietary digital recorder for all of our employees. This way, they can record notes, video, even store encrypted data, that all stays on the property."

Noah grinned. "And they'd all be linked together through the Wi-Fi network."

My father nodded.

"And they're GPS-tagged so you'd know if they leave the building," Sam added.

"All correct," my dad said. "A few of us designed the motherboard but we outsourced their construction to an outside company to save time."

"So how did they get mixed up in all this?" I asked.

My dad shook his head. "I've been back and forth with the shipping company all week," he said. "And from what I can tell, the shipment was delivered to the doorstep of the Swift *Academy* by mistake. Not Swift *Enterprises*, just across the street."

Everyone exchanged knowing glances.

"And some student found it," Sam concluded.

My dad nodded. "I think so. That's what happens when you put too many intelligent, creative kids in one place." He grinned and shrugged. "I should've seen it coming."

"What are you going to do?" I asked.

"I was thinking about asking Mr. Davenport to make an announcement," my dad replied. "See if the guilty party will just come forward."

"And if they don't?" asked Noah.

My father sighed. "I guess I'll go to the authorities." He raised an eyebrow. "Unless you intelligent, creative kids have a better idea."

I glanced around the table at my friends. Noah grinned, Sam smirked, and Amy smiled.

I slowly nodded. "If everyone here is thinking what I'm thinking, then we just might."

At lunch the next day, the four of us were eating behind the school, beside the running track. It wasn't unusual for academy students to eat lunch outside, especially if they were also testing a model rocket, enjoying a warm spring day, or setting a trap for a spybot creator.

Noah took a bite of his sandwich and glanced toward the bleachers. "Still no takers," he said.

"Give it time," I said.

Our captured spybot sat halfway up the bleachers, about twenty meters away. Noah had reassembled the goblin the night before, soldering the wires back together for the cameras and microphones. It was now fully functional as it stared out over the academy grounds.

It was also fully functional throughout the morning when we sent brief messages to the people behind the spybots. Although we had kept it sealed off in Sam's foil-lined lunch bag, we had opened the bag a few times, letting it reconnect with the Wi-Fi.

"We're so close to finding out who's behind this," Sam had said during one exchange.

"I think I can tie into this spybot and track the others down," Noah had said when the bag was opened later.

"I say we take it to my dad," I had suggested during another time the bag was opened. "I bet he can figure out how these things work."

I was particularly proud of that one. There was no way the spybot creators knew we had learned about the missing circuit boards. But they had to have known that my dad would recognize the one in their spybot immediately.

Sam dug through her plastic bowl of pasta salad. "When do you think they'll make their move?"

"Soon, I hope," Amy said. "We only have sixteen and a half minutes of lunch period left."

We had decided on placing the goblin on the bleachers since it would be extremely difficult for someone to sneak up and grab it like they did in robotics class. There were no crowds to blend with, and we could certainly identify anyone who made a move.

"Maybe they know it's a trap," Noah suggested.

"Could be," I said, glancing at the goblin, out there in the open. "But after everything we said in front of it this morning, I don't think they'll have a choice but to try to steal it back."

We continued our lunch and our watch over the lone goblin. Of everyone outside that day, no one moved close. It looked as if our plan might fail after all. Even the goblin stared back at us and seemed to say, *Ooh, look at you, thinking this plan would work.*

Sam finished her lunch and began putting her things away. "All right, Swift," she said. "What's your deal with these spybots? Why do they creep you out so much?"

I sighed and glanced around at the three faces staring back at me. Amy seemed embarrassed for me. Noah seemed intrigued. Sam pointed a finger at him. "And no ribbing."

"Hey, don't worry about me," Noah said. "After being

locked up with those things they probably creep me out more than Tom now."

"Well . . . ," I said before a long pause. My friends waited patiently while I tried to think of a way to explain it without sounding like an idiot. "I . . . uh . . . watched this old movie with my parents when I was little. It had been one of their favorites when they were younger and they wanted me to enjoy it too." I went on to describe how the monsters in the movie resembled the plastic goblins.

"Oh man. You're talking about *Gremlins*," Noah said. "That's a classic."

I jerked a little at the sound of the title. "Oh, yeah," I said. "That's it."

The name sounded right. I don't know why I couldn't think of it before. Maybe my mind was just blocking it.

"Anyway," I said. "I had so many nightmares over those creepy things."

"*Gremlins*? Really?" asked Noah. "We've seen way scarier movies than that."

Sam frowned. "Noah . . ."

Noah raised his hands. "I'm just saying. *Gremlins*?"

I frowned. "I was just a little kid. Didn't you ever get nightmares from something you saw when you were little?"

Noah shook his head. "No, man. No way."

Amy hung her head and mumbled something.

"What?" I asked her.

She let out a long breath. "*The Wizard of Oz*," she repeated. "That gave me nightmares when I was little."

Sam's eyes widened. "Me too!" She gave a dramatic shiver. "The way those flying monkeys ripped the scarecrow apart."

Noah rolled his eyes and nodded. "Okay, I might've had one or two flying-monkey nightmares back then." He looked at me seriously. "Monkeys aren't supposed to fly. You know that, right?"

Amy shook her head. "The flying monkeys didn't give me nightmares."

"They didn't?" asked Sam. "Then what did?"

Amy fidgeted with her hands. "Remember how the witch's feet stuck out from under Dorothy's house?"

"Yeah . . . ," I said.

"And remember how they curled back onto themselves once the ruby slippers were gone?" Amy asked.

"Oh, yeah," Noah said.

Amy shrugged. "*That* creeped me out. I thought they looked like two snakes."

Everyone stared at each other for a moment before bursting into laughter. Amy covered her face with embarrassment, but her shoulders bobbed up and down as she laughed, too. She let out a small snort and everyone laughed harder.

"I'm sorry, Amy," I said after I finally caught my breath. "It's not funny."

"No," Amy said with a wide grin. "It really is."

"But I got mad at you for laughing at me and . . ." I shook my head. "Actually, I think I was just mad at myself." I pointed at the goblin on the bleachers. "I felt stupid being scared of something like that."

"It's not stupid," Amy said.

"What's stupid is that I don't know how to get over it," I said.

"I bet being locked up with a bunch of them didn't help," Noah added.

I nodded. "Yeah, tell me about it."

"The gremlins in the movie must've frightened you more than you thought," Amy suggested.

"Oh yeah." I nodded. "My mom had to stay up with me every night for a whole week."

Sam cocked her head and stared at me.

"What?" I asked.

"Don't you think that's it?" she asked.

"What are you talking about?"

"Your mom was there for you the last time you saw *Gremlins*, right?" she asked. "But she's not here now. Maybe that's why these things freak you out so much."

My jaw dropped. I suddenly felt as if I had swallowed a bowling ball for lunch. I turned and stared at the goblin on the bleachers. Before, I had felt genuine fear when I looked at those things. But maybe I wasn't afraid of the toys themselves. Maybe I was afraid of what the goblins reminded me of. Maybe I was afraid of feeling the same overwhelming pain I had felt when my mother died of cancer three years ago.

"I . . ." My lower lip trembled. "I . . . think you're right."

For a long time, it was hard to think of my mother without feeling the bottomless sorrow of her loss. Only during the past year or so, I had finally gotten to a point where I could enjoy good memories of her. I no longer dwelled on just the end of her life, but all the happy times we shared before. Now, something about the appearance of the goblins had brought all that pain crashing back.

117

That and something else . . .

My eyes welled with tears as I remembered when she was sick. I remembered desperately hoping someone would find a cure for her before she died. I wasn't much of an inventor then, but I had wished someone else would've come up with something to help her. Anything. Some kind of . . .

"Lifesaving invention," I murmured.

"What?" Sam asked.

"My latest project," I explained, trying to keep my voice from cracking. "Maybe I really want so save someone's life because . . ."

Because I couldn't save hers.

My friends sat silently as I let the revelation sink in. Sam gave half a smile. Noah nodded slightly, not a wisecrack in sight, while Amy had tears forming in her own eyes. They were truly my best friends.

Suddenly, Amy glanced past me and her eyes widened. "Look out," she said as she grabbed my arm and jerked me forward.

A remote-controlled drone buzzed inches over my head. Someone must've lost control and let it get away from them. Or one of the academy students thought it would be fun to mess with some people outside during lunch.

My second theory seemed to be correct, since the drone zipped over to another group of kids enjoying a picnic lunch. They laughed as they ducked for cover. One of them even tried to swat it down with a lunchbox.

While everyone watched the drone antics, I took the opportunity to wipe my eyes. None of my friends would've made fun of me for crying, especially over something like this, but I still felt better wiping my tears in private.

I let out a breath. It was weird that my big fear of the spybots wasn't actually about them at all. Sure, they were a little creepy, but now I knew what I was really feeling when I looked at them. And knowing that kind of took their power away.

I turned to gaze at the goblin. That feeling of dread was still there, but it felt . . . smaller, somehow. More under control.

As I stared at the bleachers, I saw someone creeping up toward the toy. A tall boy, wearing a hoodie. He ran up the bleachers, his long legs letting him take the steps two at a time as he scrambled straight for the spybot.

Now I saw the drone for what it was—a diversion. I sprang to my feet and sprinted toward him.

I reached the bottom of the bleachers just as the figure reached the goblin.

"Hey!" I shouted. "Leave that alone!"

The guy turned at the sound of my voice. It was a fellow student—Jim Mills. Oddly enough, though, he didn't stop. He stared at me with wide eyes as he desperately reached for the spybot.

Unfortunately, Jim didn't watch where he was going and overshot the goblin completely. I felt as if I were watching the entire thing in slow motion as Jim's hand missed the toy and overextended the edge of the bleachers. I leaped onto the bottom bleacher, trying to get to him in time, but I didn't have a chance. Jim's momentum carried him forward, tumbling over the side, and then onto the ground below.

Jim cried out in pain as he smacked the ground. I cringed and hopped off the bleachers, running around to join him. Noah, Sam, and Amy rushed up next, followed by the rest of the surrounding students. We gathered around Jim as he cringed and held his left leg.

"I'll get Ms. Ramos," Amy announced before dashing toward the school.

"Jim Mills?" Noah asked. "You're the guy?"

"Are you all right, man?" asked one of the students. It was Jim's friend, Jason Hammond, and he held an RC controller in one hand. The kind that might control a drone, maybe.

"I think I . . . broke my ankle," Jim grunted.

I grabbed Noah's shoulder. "Go get my backpack."

"On it," Noah said, before pushing through the crowd.

I looked up at Jason. "So you guys created the spy-bots?"

The assembled crowd grumbled with a mixture of approval and disapproval.

Jason nodded. "Yeah, it was going to be our internship project," he said. "But things kind of got out of hand."

"Dude," Jim scolded between winces.

Jason shrugged. "It's over, man. That's what I've been trying to tell you."

"If you wanted my father's attention, you definitely have it," I said.

"Yeah, man," Noah agreed as he pushed back through the crowd. "He could've called the cops on you."

I unzipped my backpack and dug past my laptop, tablet, jacket . . . I'm not the best when it comes to putting things away, so I hoped that I still had what I was looking for. When my hand fell on crinkly plastic, I knew I was good. I pulled out a clear plastic tube with a little CO_2 canister attached.

"Help me lift his leg," I told Noah.

As we carefully lifted his leg, I slowly slid the plastic sleeve over it.

"Whoa, what are you doing?" asked Jim.

I pointed up to Jason. "I need a battery."

"What?" Jason asked.

I nodded to his hands. "The battery in your controller?"

"Oh, right," Jason said as he pulled out the nine-volt battery from his RC controller.

Jim grunted again. "What are you doing?"

"Remember my airbag suit?" I asked.

Jim gave me a puzzled look. "Yeah?"

"This was a spare piece for one of the legs," I explained. "If I can get this to inflate, it should make a nice splint." I found the two lead wires and moved them toward the battery leads.

"Whoa, wait a minute," Jim said.

"Are you sure about this, Swift?" Sam asked.

"Hey, it was Ms. Ramos's idea," I said.

I touched the wires to the battery, triggering the canister. The clear tube inflated around Jim's leg in an instant.

"How does that feel?" I asked him.

Jim nodded slowly. "A little better. Thanks."

"Okay, make a hole, people," Ms. Ramos said as she pushed through the crowd. The onlookers parted and the school nurse appeared with a large orange bag hanging over her shoulder. She knelt beside Jim. "What do we have?"

"He fell off the bleachers," I said.

"The same leg, Ms. Ramos," Jim added.

Of course. Jim had been one of her patients before. He was the one who gave her that first spybot.

14
The Restitution
Solution

"AW, MAN," NOAH SAID AS HE SCROLLED THROUGH his phone. "Do you know how many first-aid apps there are already?"

"I give up," I conceded. "How many?"

"Too many," Noah said as he slid his phone back into his pocket. "So much for my programming contribution to the medical world."

We exited the front doors and trotted down the school's main steps. Noah was going home with me again and we were meeting my dad at Swift Enterprises.

After the now-infamous bleacher incident, Noah was

all on board with coming up with a lifesaving invention. Of course, being the programmer that he was, his first thought was a cool first-aid phone app.

"Okay, hear me out," Noah said. "You know those neck braces the EMTs use? What if you cut down one of your leg sections and made an inflatable version of that? Just push a button and . . ."

"And instantly choke the person you're trying to save?" I asked.

Noah nodded. "Okay, that idea is still a little rough around the edges. I get it."

We stopped at the crosswalk and waited for a break in the line of cars picking up students. One of the parents waved us on, and we hurried across to the main walkway, crossing the Swift Enterprises parking lot. Sharp footsteps grew louder as someone hurried behind us.

"Tom, Noah," greeted Ms. Ramos as she fell into step beside us.

"Hi, Ms. Ramos," we replied.

"What are you doing here?" asked Noah.

"Oh, just following up with a patient," she replied with a sly grin. "And you?"

"My dad's running late," I explained. "He has to get the new interns started today."

She nodded. "I see."

We entered the building and Noah and I turned over our backpacks to the security desk. Ms. Ramos did the same with her phone and we were all issued visitor badges. I led the way toward the main elevator.

"Fourth floor, please," Ms. Ramos asked.

I smiled up at her and pressed the button. "Us too."

Once on the fourth floor, we made our way to one of the Swift Enterprises clean rooms. It was a completely dust-free environment where employees could work on sensitive electronic components without the possibility of contamination. Since the rooms were completely sealed, we went to a nearby observation room. I knocked on the door and peeked through the small window. One of my father's employees, McKee Smith, waved us in.

The small room consisted of a single desk, a chair, and a large window separating the clean room.

"Hi, Mr. Smith," I said.

"Hey, Tom, Noah," Mr. Smith said before getting to his feet. "And hi, Jessica. What brings you here?"

Ms. Ramos nodded to the large window. "Just checking up on my patient."

On the other side of the glass, Jim and Jason worked at a small table in a stark white room. They both wore white plastic jumpsuits with hoods that covered almost every part of their bodies.

Jim and Jason had kind of guaranteed their places in the Swift Enterprises internship program, although it wasn't what they thought it would be. You see, someone had to dismantle all those spybots. They each had one of the little goblins in front of them as they carefully removed the components. Stacks of clear plastic bins lined the wall behind them, each filled with dozens of the little spybots.

Mr. Smith pointed to a red button mounted on the desk. It sat under a thin microphone. "Press that to talk to them."

Ms. Ramos pressed the button and leaned forward. "How are you doing, Jim?"

Jim looked up from his work and his voice emanated from a small speaker on the wall. "I'm okay, thanks." His bandaged ankle was wrapped in clear plastic and his two crutches were propped nearby.

The office door opened and my dad walked in. He pointed to the clean room. "See, Jessica? I promised I'd keep him off his feet."

It turned out that Jim didn't break his leg at all. He'd just sprained his ankle. Unfortunately for him, it was the one that he had strained earlier in the week. Ms. Ramos had wrapped it for him then, but when he fell off the bleachers, she sent him to the emergency room for X-rays just to be sure.

My dad reached over and pressed the button. "How's it going, guys?"

"Fine, sir," they both replied.

"How many have you removed so far?"

Jim pointed to a small tray on the table. "Three, sir." Three circuit boards sat upright in the rack, each in a clear antistatic pouch. Jim and Jason found out the hard way that it takes much longer to melt the connecting solder and remove components properly—without damaging the sophisticated circuitry on the expensive circuit boards.

"Oh man," I whispered. "That's going to take forever."

"Don't do the crime if you can't do the time," said Noah.

"When I was in the army, they had us peel potatoes," Mr. Smith said with a chuckle.

All of us tried very hard not to laugh. Even though they couldn't hear us, they could certainly see us.

My dad turned his back to the window and crossed his arms. "Well, I'm not telling them this now, but I was genuinely impressed with their spybot design."

"I agree," said Mr. Smith. "The ear design really picked up the slightest sound."

Noah rolled his eyes. "Tell me about it."

"Well . . ." My dad glanced around. "Since they're so familiar with the circuit boards, I'm going to have them assemble and test the new recorders." He shrugged. "Maybe even throw out some design ideas."

Ms. Ramos smiled. "They'll love that."

I looked through the window and noticed a small bin with three empty goblin shells. I leaned over and pressed the button.

"Can I have one of those plastic goblins?" I asked.

Jason shrugged. "Dude, you can have as many as you want."

"Just one," I replied. "Thanks."

"No problem," Jason said as he grabbed two halves of

a goblin. "I'll pass one through." He assembled it, using the magnet to hold them together, and dropped it in a special drawer in the wall.

I caught Noah's eye as he stared at me in disbelief. "What?" I asked him.

"I thought those things creeped you out," he said.

"They used to," I said as I opened the drawer. I grabbed the empty goblin. It felt much lighter in my hands. "Now it just reminds me of something else."

Noah didn't press the issue. He knew exactly what I was talking about.

I turned the little figurine over in my hands. It stared back up at me with its wide eyes and circular mouth. Its expression didn't seem so devious anymore. In fact, it almost looked as if it were saying, *Ooh, look at you, growing up a little.*

DON'T MISS TOM'S NEXT ADVENTURE!
- Augmented Reality -

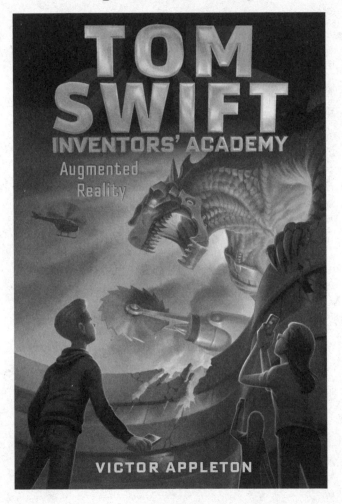